PERSONA IN STRATA

PERSONA IN STRATA

TOBIAS MALM

ISBN: 978-91-531-2666-9 (Paperback)
Published by Tobias Malm
www.tobiasmalm.com

This is a work of fiction. All characters and events in this novel are products of the author's imagination. Any resemblance to real persons, living or dead, or actual events is purely coincidental. Public agencies, institutions, and historical figures mentioned are used solely to provide context for the fictional characters and their actions

PREFACE

I NEVER THOUGHT I would become a whistleblower. Until yesterday, the very notion would have been laughable. *A traitor?* Certainly not. I was a patriot, willing to do anything for my country. The idea of disclosing classified information to the public wouldn't have crossed my mind. That wasn't who I was. But the information I've uncovered is simply too vital to remain concealed. Make no mistake, my loyalty to my country remains steadfast, and my actions are guided by the best interests of my fellow citizens. However, this issue is far too urgent to be left to the slow grind of bureaucracy.

I wish I had more time to weigh all the factors and meticulously plan my next move, but regrettably, I have only a few days at most. Strangely enough, my grasp on the concept of time has become distorted. I struggle to even comprehend its meaning. It has morphed into an enigma, a notion that eludes me. What I do know is that a narrow window of opportunity lies before me. Despite the life-threatening risks, I must seize it. Our very existence hinges on my actions. This disclosure isn't driven by idealism, nor is it about freedom, constitutional rights, or democracy. It's about survival—nothing more, nothing less. And I need your help. I implore you to read the following account and determine what you're willing to do to support me. The following statement may sound preposterous, but it remains true: an event took place sixty-six million years ago, and I need your help to stop it.

THE TESTIMONY

I WAS IN THE middle of an invertebrate excavation in Coahuila when my phone rang. After hours under the relentless sun, the call was a welcome break. I brushed the dust off my hands and reached for my phone. The noise from the nearby highway—known locally as the Carretera Interoceánica—made it hard to hear the caller at first.

"Sorry, I can't—" I started, cupping my hand against my ear. "Who is this?"

"As I said, I'm Lieutenant-Colonel Kira Calder from the Response Unit."

I wiped the sweat from my forehead with a dirty cloth. "What's that?"

"Are you Dr. Ian Foster, the paleontologist?"

"Yeah," I replied, still baffled. "Did you say Response Unit?"

"It's the Canadian Joint Incident Response Unit."

"I don't think I've heard of—"

"It's a sub-unit of the Canadian Special Operations Forces Command."

My head started to spin. I needed water. *Special Operations Forces?* I tried to grasp what they could possibly want with me. "How can I help?"

"It's a matter of national security, and we believe your expertise could be crucial," the voice on the other end continued.

"I regret that I can't share more details over the phone, but I assure you, your involvement is essential. If you agree to assist us in this urgent matter, we'll have a plane ready for you at Plan de Guadalupe International Airport within two days. This transport will take you to a confidential location, where you'll receive a more detailed briefing."

I glanced at my colleagues, toiling in the relentless heat, as I tried to process what I'd just heard. "Listen," I said, hesitating. "We're doing important work here, and we're nowhere near finished. You'll need to give me more information if you expect me to just up and leave. I'm the senior—"

"It's up to you," Kira said. "But this should interest you a great deal. And of course, you'll be compensated for your service."

"And you can't tell me anything more than that?" I asked.

"All I can say, Doctor, is that there's been a discovery."

"Huh..." I paused, my curiosity suddenly piqued. I thought about my responsibilities to my team. Just this morning, they were my driving force, but now they felt like shackles. I didn't know what to say, but the words came out as if on autopilot: "Plan de Guadalupe, on Wednesday?"

After the phone call, I had to sit down. Taking off my hat, I opened a bottle of water, poured some over my head, and drank the rest. My team glanced at me with concern as they continued their work around the dig site. *A discovery?* I couldn't begin to fathom what kind of discovery would require the involvement of both the military and a paleontologist. My pulse was racing, and it wasn't just from the sweltering heat. I was worried, but I couldn't deny the excitement creeping in as well. Focusing on my work for the rest of the day was nearly impossible. By the end of it, I felt embarrassed having to lie to my team, telling them I needed to go home because of family matters. They were clearly puzzled—everyone knew I wasn't exactly a family man—but they had no choice but to respect my decision not to discuss it further. I felt guilty leaving them like this. They'd have to halt the work until they could find someone to replace me, which was a real setback given the limited time we had at this site. But I had to go. The woman on the phone had been right—whatever they had discovered intrigued me too much to ignore.

As soon as I stepped off the plane at Pearson Airport, I was immediately escorted to a military vehicle. It drove me a short distance—no more than half a kilometer—to a camouflaged helicopter waiting on an old, unused helipad at the edge of the airport. Armed guards stood watch around it. Kira, who turned out to be slightly younger than me, helped strap me in and took a seat next to me. Across from us sat an elderly man in full uniform—a general. He wore black sunglasses, but I could still sense his gaze fixed on me. I leaned forward and offered my hand. He smiled, giving me a firm handshake.

"I'm Ian!" I shouted, struggling to be heard over the roar of the rotor blades as they began to spin above us.

"You don't have to yell," came the general's voice through my headset, calm and clear. "I know who you are. I'm Jordan Simmons." He pointed at my hat and added with a grin, "That's a nice hat. You look like quite the adventurer with that on. Fitting for the occasion." He winked and then turned to Kira. "You didn't tell him yet, did you?"

"No, sir," Kira replied.

"Tell me what?" I asked, still anxious to know. The helicopter was lifting off now, and I could feel the ground slipping away beneath us. "I don't even know where we're going."

"She didn't even tell you that?" Jordan said, a smirk playing on his lips. "Well, what we're dealing with is top secret, so we can't share any details until you've been given proper clearance and signed the NDA. We'll handle all of that once we arrive at the site, so don't worry. But I can at least tell you where we're headed. The site is in Yukon, near the border."

"Are the Americans involved?" I asked.

Jordan laughed. "No, but by now they've probably noticed our recent activity in the area, so our goal is to get this done as quickly as possible. That's where you come in. You'll be briefed at the site, so just sit back and relax for now."

Relax? I was baffled. My mind started racing with far-fetched ideas, the kind I would never have entertained if it weren't for the military presence and their cloak of secrecy. The idea that intrigued me the most, and seemed the most plausible among my otherwise implausible thoughts, was that they had discovered a living specimen of a prehistoric species and needed me to identify it. *A living dinosaur*? The thought was absurd, of course, but undeniably thrilling. As a child, I had often fantasized about seeing a living dinosaur, and now, just the possibility of it made me feel like a little kid again.

We landed in a field in the middle of nowhere. The chill in the air hit me immediately, made worse by the fact that I wasn't dressed for the cold.

"You'll get some warmer clothes when we arrive," Jordan said as we stood outside the helicopter, waiting.

He pulled out a half-smoked cigar from his breast pocket and lit it. In the distance, a military jeep appeared, growing larger as it approached. The sun was sinking behind the snow-capped mountains, and with each passing minute, the world around us grew darker. The jeep switched on its headlights, and by the time it arrived, the stars had already begun to dot the sky. My heartbeat quickened with each passing mile as we drew closer to our destination. I pictured the so-called site as a temporary base of operations, complete with military tents and some kind of storage unit where they were keeping the discovery.

I was wrong. About two hours later, we arrived at a recently abandoned construction site deep in the boreal forest. The military personnel—only around thirty men and women—were making use of the facilities left behind by the construction workers.

"You'll sign all the necessary papers now," Kira said. "After that, you'll be shown to the barracks where you'll meet the rest of the team. You'll all be briefed in the morning."

After I had signed the mountain of papers, I was shown to the barrack where the rest of my team was staying. They were already asleep in their bunks, so any introductions would have to wait until morning. As I sneaked inside, trying not to wake anyone, I counted four people. Satisfied that I hadn't disturbed them, I quietly settled into my own bunk. My head was spinning with questions, making it impossible to fall asleep, and just when I finally felt ready to doze off, Jordan opened the door, letting in the light of dawn.

"Howdy!" he said, a new cigar between his lips and a friendly grin on his face. "Please get dressed and step outside. I'll brief you on the way to the location."

Kira stood next to him, holding some papers in her hand. I was the first to join them outside the barrack. The air was chilly, my breath evaporating in the cool air, but the morning sun provided a faint warmth. A few armed guards patrolled the area in the distance, and I could hear the faint sound of radio chatter coming from their direction.

The next person to come out of the barrack was a slightly overweight young man—perhaps in his twenties—with a rather pale complexion and a faded t-shirt with a locomotive on it.

He stretched and yawned before addressing me, avoiding direct eye contact.

"I'm Rodney Timbrell," he said, scratching his chin with his finger. "I like trains."

"I'm Ian," I replied, "and, uh, I like dinosaurs."

Rodney immediately looked me in the eye and smiled. "What's your favorite dinosaur?" he asked with surprising enthusiasm in his otherwise robotic voice. "I like dinosaurs, too."

"I—I'm," I started, caught off guard by his sudden shift in demeanor. "I'm sorry, but what's your profession—I mean, why did they bring you here?"

"Um," he muttered, once again avoiding eye contact, "I'm currently unemployed. I don't really know why they brought me here, but they said it was a matter of national security." He snorted. "You should have seen Mom's face when they told her."

"Really?" I said, still flabbergasted. "But—"

I was interrupted by a woman around my age stepping out of the barrack, shielding her eyes from the morning sun with her hand. She introduced herself as Shun Chen. For a moment, I feared she might also have some unexpected role here, but to my relief, she turned out to be a paleontologist, just like me. A few moments later, two more people joined us outside—Stefan Williams and Miguel Boisclair, both archaeologists rather than paleontologists. I recognized Stefan from a conference in Vienna a few years back, but he didn't seem to recognize me.

This team composition pretty much shattered my childish dream of seeing a living dinosaur. It became clear that we weren't here because of my expertise in prehistory, but because of our experience in carefully digging things up from the ground. I felt a bit ridiculous for even entertaining those far-out ideas. Disappointment crept in as well. *Was this just a mundane excavation?*

"Okay!" Jordan said, clapping his hands together before heading into the surrounding forest. Kira looked a bit surprised but swiftly caught up to him. "Come on, let's get going," Jordan continued. "We don't have all day."

We all followed.

"What do you think they've found?" Shun whispered to me.

"I have no idea, to be honest," I replied, reluctant to share the wild ideas I'd entertained earlier. "It's probably some military equipment, maybe an aircraft or a weapon—"

"Two weeks ago, the construction workers at this site accidentally unearthed something," Jordan said as we continued walking. "It's the kind of thing you wouldn't believe if I just told you, so I'm going to show you. It's not dangerous, so no need to be alarmed. It's just… Well, it's strange. Frankly, I'm hoping you'll be able to give me a better explanation than I can give you. Perhaps it's nothing, and we can all go home tomorrow."

We arrived at a clearing where the construction workers had just begun digging the foundation for a building. The military had set up a camouflaged tent over the hole, and three armed guards stood watch around it. The sight made me feel uneasy.

"Come on," Jordan said, gesturing with his cigar. "Step forward and look down this hole."

The hole wasn't deep, but it had reached the bedrock. At first glance, nothing seemed out of the ordinary.

"You can't see it, can you?" Jordan said. "It's small, and I bet it's too unexpected for your brains to even consider the pattern. But it's there. Look at the corner." He pointed with his cigar. "Look carefully."

We all gathered at the corner of the hole and peered down. It wasn't obvious at first, but once we were told to look for something unusual, it only took a few seconds to spot it. Rodney was the first to speak:

"Those are train wheels."

"That's what it looks like," Jordan said. "Train wheels. Or to be more precise, fossilized train wheels."

The pattern was unmistakable—two train wheels, seen from the side. I didn't know what to think.

"Not fossilized," Stefan corrected. "Fossils refer to preserved organic material, which this isn't. Still, it could've formed through similar processes... Might be an imprint, an impression in the rock, or perhaps a result of some kind of permineralization. I suppose the former could've happened fairly recently under the right conditions, although I've never heard of it happening before."

"What other alternatives are there?" Miguel scoffed. "The bedrock doesn't look like something that formed recently, though. I'd bet it's the work of a hoaxer, like those guys who faked giant penguin tracks back in the forties. It caused a big stir, and the media fell for it pretty hard."

"The construction workers didn't just dig this hole and find the train wheels like this," Kira explained. "They removed a layer of the bedrock and found this underneath. Unless someone managed to carve the inside of the rock, these remains are genuine."

"Or the construction workers removed a piece of rock that had been placed on top of it," Shun countered. "I mean, what you're suggesting here is impossible. Any other explanation is better."

Jordan let out a sigh. "We know this is real. Before we decided to bring you here, we removed more of the rock layer—albeit a bit unprofessionally—and revealed more of the wheels. So, no one has carved this pattern into the rock."

"But sir," I began hesitantly, "this is the kind of rock we've found dinosaurs in, close to Alberta. To my eyes, it looks to be millions of years old. I can't say anything for sure without a closer examination, but I'm pretty confident that—"

"Before we brought you here," Jordan interrupted, "we had some of the rocks sent to a lab for dating. I'm no expert, but… Kira, help me out here, would you?"

"Sir, they used radiometric dating methods," she explained.

"And?" Shun asked. "How old is it?"

"It's—" Kira cleared her throat, as if struggling to believe the words she was about to say. "It's approximately sixty-six million years old."

Shun crouched down, putting her hands on her forehead in disbelief. I felt the same way… I think we all did. A heavy silence hung in the air until Jordan finally broke it.

"It's a tough nut to crack," he said, taking a puff on his cigar. "That's why we brought you here. We suspect there's an entire train car hidden beneath the rock. And we need you to unearth it for us."

"It's a subway!" Rodney exclaimed with a huge smile, scratching his face excessively. "The wheel arrangement hints at an electric train, most likely a subway car considering the size."

Everyone stared at him.

"You can tell that just from this small part of the—" Jordan began.

"Yes!" Rodney interrupted, still grinning. "I can tell."

"Well, there you go!" Jordan said, sounding impressed. "I must admit I was skeptical about bringing you on board instead of a professional, but you're already proving yourself useful. Is there anything more you can say about this train?"

"N-no," Rodney stammered, his expression shifting to one of concern as he began to rock back and forth slightly.

Shun reached out to calm him, gently touching his arm.

"Don't touch me," Rodney said, stepping back abruptly before turning and walking away.

"Kira?" Jordan said, prompting her to nod and follow Rodney back to the barracks.

"No one in Canada knows more about trains than Rodney," Jordan continued. "He can identify any train from just seeing a tiny part of it. But, as you might have noticed, he's a bit challenged. We all need to be calm around him, and for the love of God, don't touch him. He hates that."

All of this was difficult to digest, to say the least. A preserved subway car from sixty-six million years ago? Even with the convincing evidence, I still couldn't bring myself to fully believe it.

Back in the barrack, I sat on the edge of my bed, trying to make sense of it all. Rodney paced back and forth, scratching his cheek and mumbling something to himself. Stefan stood in the doorway, gazing out at the landscape, lost in thought.

Miguel, rummaging through his backpack, asked Stefan to close the door to keep the cold out. For a while, none of us spoke, each of us lost in our own thoughts, trying to process what we had just witnessed. I didn't know what to believe. Clearly, there were no trains sixty-six million years ago—certainly not a train that a modern enthusiast could recognize—but I couldn't deny what I had just seen. The silence was finally broken when Shun, having just returned from the outhouse outside the barracks, stepped in and spoke.

"Are we being pranked?" Shun asked. "I mean, this is completely insane!"

"I'm leaving," Miguel announced, apparently packing his bag. "It must be some damn TV show. I have to admit it's a fun idea—presenting a fictional mystery to a bunch of experts to see how they solve it. But I don't want to be here when they jump out with the cameras!"

"Do you really think they would involve the military in something like that?" Stefan asked. "I don't believe—"

"How do you know it's not just a bunch of actors?" Miguel shot back.

"Jordan Simmons was interviewed on the news a while ago," Stefan pointed out. "So he's not an actor, at least."

"In that case, it's some sort of psychological experiment!" Miguel huffed, his irritation flaring. "The audacity to drag us here like this. I have a pregnant wife back home."

"What could they possibly gain from such an experiment?" I asked. "It doesn't seem very likely to me."

"Likely? Don't you understand what they're trying to make us believe?" Miguel scoffed. "They're suggesting that the train car traveled back in time. Or maybe they want us to buy into some ancient civilization nonsense." He laughed, a mix of disbelief and frustration. "Likely? Any theory we come up with that doesn't involve time travel or ancient civilizations from the Cretaceous period is going to be more likely."

"I don't think they're trying to deceive us," Stefan said. "However, I wouldn't be surprised if they messed up the dating. Incompetence is probably the best explanation. The train car must have ended up underground much more recently."

"We need to request access to the results of their dating of the bedrock," Shun suggested. "If we're allowed to see those, we can determine whether a mistake was made."

"Nonsense," Miguel said. "Incompetent or not, I feel tricked."

"Give it a chance," Stefan urged. "If you leave now, you'll never find out what it was all about."

"What do you say, Rodney?" Shun asked.

"What does he know?" Miguel dismissed him with a wave.

Rodney paused, gathering his thoughts. "It's a modern subway car; it can't have been there long enough to look like that, at least not if it's been there since sometime after it was built. Either it's been there longer than what's possible, or someone deliberately tried to make it look that way. We could rule out the latter the same way Jordan claims they did—by checking if there's more of the car under the undisturbed rock."

"There are too many ifs," Miguel said, shaking his head. "And we can't just take your word for it, Rodney. The train might be an old mine car that just happens to look like a modern subway. But okay, you've convinced me—I'll stay the week. Not because I'm actually considering time travel or whatever, but because I want to prove that I'm right!"

I didn't share Miguel's temperament, but I did share his skepticism. We all probably did to a degree. The idea of a living dinosaur hiding in the Yukon wilderness would have been more believable than this. I wasn't a physicist, but I knew enough to understand that time travel wasn't possible. If Rodney was mistaken, the remains might conceivably belong to an extinct civilization built by an unknown intelligent species, but as Miguel pointed out, even that seemed highly improbable.

We continued our speculations in the cramped confines of the barrack, going around in circles since we couldn't reach any satisfying conclusions without examining the train wheels ourselves. As a result, we eagerly awaited Jordan and his team to prepare all the equipment we needed to begin the excavation—which, fortunately, took only a couple of hours.

With unlimited funding, the dig was a dream come true for us. We didn't have to worry about the usual limitations or administrative hurdles, and the mystery surrounding the find only added to the excitement. But it was hard work—probably the hardest I've ever done in the field. We were short-staffed, due to the general's order to keep as few people in the know as possible, and the cold weather took its toll on us. Our hands were stiff, and the dirt was nearly as hard as the bedrock. It would have been wiser to wait for summer, but it was clear that Jordan was in a hurry.

Shun was the first to uncover another part of the subway car; it was far enough from the initial finding that a mine car, like Miguel had suggested, could be ruled out. Miguel remained as skeptical as ever, perhaps even more so, but my own uncertainty only grew. Shun managed to convince Jordan to show us the results of the dating. They had done a thorough job, sending samples to several different laboratories, all of which had reached the same conclusion: sixty-six million years old. A shiver ran down my spine as I looked at the results, and when I met Shun's eyes, I could see she felt the same.

"What does this mean?" I asked as we sat in the barrack. "The dating is accurate, and it's clearly a subway car, or at least some kind of train car. And there have probably never been any tracks here."

"It's a hoax," Miguel insisted, still refusing to entertain the more astounding possibilities. "Someone has done a very good job making it look realistic, that's all."

"An incredibly good job, in that case," Stefan remarked.

"An impossible one," Shun added. "How do you suppose they chiseled the pattern under the upper rock layer without removing it?"

"They must have used some form of radiation," Miguel suggested. "It may sound incredible—"

"Someone making their way all the way out here with a mysterious radioactive device is definitely something I would classify as incredible," Shun retorted.

"And yet it's more likely than someone traveling back to the Cretaceous period and dumping a train car!" Miguel exclaimed. "Besides, it might be possible to achieve what I'm suggesting in some simpler way than radiation; that was just an example. But anything is more believable than a damn time traveler!"

"It could still be a remnant from some extinct civilization,"

I said, entertaining the idea once again. "We haven't confirmed that it's a subway car yet. Haven't any of you heard of the Silurian hypothesis? It's more of a thought experiment than a hypothesis, really. If there was an industrial civilization before humanity, could we find evidence of it in the geological record? This find might answer that question."

"It's a subway car," said Rodney, who had been lying on his bed staring up at the ceiling until now. "And even if it's not, it's still a modern train car. The probability that another civilization would have constructed a train exactly like ours is extremely small. I therefore believe we can rule out the Silurian hypothesis as an explanation for this."

"But traveling back in time," I said. "That's not even physically possible, is it?"

Rodney, like a tape recorder, launched into a lengthy explanation: "The theory of relativity claims that time is not absolute, which might potentially allow time to bend to such a degree that a loop is formed—something that could possibly permit travel back in time. Wormholes, so-called Einstein-Rosen bridges, have also been suggested as a method of traveling back in time. Additionally, there are theories that cosmic strings, by moving parallel to each other at high speeds, could make time travel possible. The Many-Worlds interpretation of quantum mechanics might also enable a form of time travel, but in that case, only through alternative timelines. Or perhaps the simulation hypothesis is true, which could allow time travel by rewinding the simulation to a previous state or by sending someone in the simulation to a new simulation of an earlier state of the prior simulation." He spoke faster and faster, scratching his belly as he went on. "However, the simulation hypothesis has been criticized for being unscientific and strictly philosophical, which many consider as—"

"Thank you, Rodney," Shun interjected, stopping him. "Even if time travel is possible, why would anyone choose to send a subway car sixty-six million years back in time, to Yukon of all places?"

We fell silent. No one knew what to say. No matter how we looked at it, the answer seemed equally absurd.

"Where do you usually work?" I asked, looking down at Shun during a break. She was the only other paleontologist here, so we often ended up working closely together. I held a steaming cup of coffee in my hand as I spoke. She looked up at me, brushing some sweaty strands of hair away from her face.

"Could you pass me that brush over there?" She pointed to one of the brushes, smiling a crooked smile that made me smile back more genuinely than usual. I tossed the brush to her, and she caught it effortlessly. "I lecture at the University of Ontario," she continued. "When I'm not doing fieldwork, that is."

I told her where I worked, then asked, "Why do you think they chose you specifically, I mean for this? I have no idea why they picked me."

"We're competent enough to dig this up," she said, "but not well-known enough in the field to be trusted if we decided to talk about it. Beyond that, it's probably just a coincidence they chose us specifically. They don't want our expertise; they just want this out of the ground as quickly as possible."

I took a sip of my coffee. "You're probably right about that. Do you think they know more about this than they're letting on?"

Shun carefully brushed dirt from the surface we were uncovering. "I don't think they know much more than we do. They brought Rodney here because they couldn't even identify the type of train."

"That's true," I agreed, taking another sip of my coffee. "Well, I guess it's time to get back to work."

I put away the coffee and jumped down into the pit, shovel in hand. "When they called me, I actually thought they had found a living dinosaur," I admitted with a smile as I struggled to dig up some frozen soil.

Shun laughed, but not in a mocking way. I tried to suppress a grin. "What about you?" I asked, "What did you think it was about when the military called you?"

"I assumed they'd found some fossils on one of their bases," she said. "After all, they have the same responsibility as anyone else to halt their work to avoid damaging a find and to contact the authorities. But I did find it odd that they contacted me directly instead of going through the university. That was the only thing that made me suspect something was off."

I got down on my knees and started clearing away some larger chunks of dirt. "Yeah, that was definitely a more realistic assumption than mine. I guess my wishful thinking got the better of me. Seeing a living dinosaur has been a dream of mine since childhood. Did you have any dreams like that?"

"My interest in paleontology was sparked in my teenage years when a relative mentioned that the inspiration for dragons might have come from dinosaur skeletons. My mom bought me an old book about dinosaurs, filled with, admittedly outdated, illustrations, and from that point on, I was hooked. But I never really entertained the idea of seeing a living dinosaur. It wasn't just the animals themselves that fascinated me—it was also the time they lived in. The thought that the Earth once looked so different… that idea has always captured my imagination."

Feeling a bit bashful, I admitted, "For me, it all started when

I saw *Jurassic Park* in the theater when I was eight years old. I thought dinosaurs were the coolest thing ever, and I'd run around pretending to be a Velociraptor. The neighbors must have thought I was developmentally challenged."

Shun laughed again, her gaze lingering on me a little longer than I'd expected. A slight blush crept onto my cheeks, making me look down at the ground. "That movie probably sparked more interest in paleontology than anything before it," Shun said, "but I personally preferred *The Land Before Time.*"

I raised my eyes to meet hers again. There was something fragile in her gaze, I thought, but also something sharp. Already, I found myself not wanting to lose contact with her after our work here was finished, but I couldn't tell if she felt the same way.

About three months in, while uncovering one of the windows in the middle section of the train car, we began to notice something truly disturbing. It was a passenger—the only one we would find. The figure was barely visible, just a partially eroded face peering straight at us through where the glass would have been, twisted into an expression of agony. As we excavated more of this section, we could see that the person was holding something up against the window. All we could discern about the object was that it was rectangular in shape. Any details that might have indicated what it was had long since eroded away. We stood around the face in a circle, silently staring at it.

"Well, I'll be damned," Jordan finally said, lighting a cigar. "A person. It doesn't look like he wanted to be there." He paused, glancing at Kira, who stood next to him. "Do you think this changes things?"

"I wonder who it was," Shun said. "Could it really be a time traveler?"

Time travel, as bizarre as it seemed, had gradually become our working theory—though Miguel remained skeptical, unwilling to embrace the idea. Despite our growing suspicions, Jordan had remained tight-lipped about his own theories. It wasn't until now, as we stood staring at the tormented face buried in the ground, that he finally shared some of his thoughts.

"An involuntary time traveler," he said. "This *does* change things."

"What aren't you telling us?" I pressed. "We need to be in the loop if you want us to do our job properly—"

"Couldn't they have used the train car—" Stefan started.

"As a time machine?" Jordan interrupted. "This isn't *Back to the Future*. No one would choose a subway car as their vehicle of choice for time travel. Somehow, this happened by accident. And, frankly, that worries me."

He stormed off, and a few minutes later, we could hear him yelling into the phone inside his barrack. We couldn't make out what he was saying, but it was clear he was agitated.

We continued digging for another three months before anything significant happened. Early one morning, Shun called out my name. She was working on what appeared to be the front of the subway car. I walked over to her and asked what was going on.

"I just removed some rock matrix here," she said. "And, well, take a look. What do you see?"

"Oh, my God," I said, "are those letters?"

There were three letters, with spaces between them.

"Bingo. The first one is B."

The other two letters weren't capitalized: "h" and "z."

"I think it spelled a word once, but some of the letters are missing," Shun said.

"That would mean—" I began, but then a shadow fell over us. We looked up to see Rodney standing there, a huge smile on his face.

"Oh," Shun said, surprised. "Hey, Rodney."

"Hey!" Rodney exclaimed. "Those are letters."

"Yes, they are," Shun replied. "Do they mean anything to you?"

He began scratching his chin, clearly excited. "Yes."

"What?" I asked.

"Subway cars often have serial numbers or other types of designations, like names," Rodney explained.

"Right," Shun said. Then, lowering her voice, she added, "Rodney, can you make me a promise?"

"Yes." His smile grew even wider.

"Don't tell anyone about this. Not Miguel, not Stefan, not Kira, and especially not Jordan."

"Wait," I interrupted. "What's going on?"

Without answering, Shun picked up her rock hammer and smashed it down on the letters, obliterating them.

"Whoa!" I exclaimed. "What are you—"

"Shh," she hissed. "Don't you understand?"

"What?" I said, still in shock. "You just damaged the most important discovery ever made!"

"Time travel," Rodney chimed in, grinning.

I looked up at him, more confused than ever.

"Look, Ian…" Shun began. "What do you think will happen when we're done here?"

"I—I don't know, but—"

"They'll fly this thing to some secret base, and that'll be the last we ever see of it. We'll be sent home, forced to keep quiet or risk being locked away in some maximum-security prison for the criminally insane. We're just the dig team."

I began to see her point, though I was still hesitant to fully grasp it.

"Right now, somewhere in the world, and for some unknown reason," she said, "there's a subway car that, at some point in time, will travel back sixty-six million years. And those letters might be the only clue to figuring out which one it is."

"You don't know that," I countered. "It might have already happened, or it might not happen for another hundred years."

"True," Shun acknowledged. "But don't you want to know for sure?"

"Say we find it," I said. "What do you suggest we do then?"

There was a brief silence before Rodney's robotic voice broke through again from above:

"Time travel."

Shun had been right. After we unearthed the subway car, we helped them fly it out of there and were sent home without any acknowledgment whatsoever. They interviewed Rodney every time we uncovered a new part, but he never mentioned the letters. He seemed to relish keeping the secret, feeling as if he was part of our little group. And he was. After spending six months working so closely together, the dig team—including Rodney—felt a bit like family.

Back at home, I missed that sense of camaraderie. The only person I stayed in contact with was Shun. By this point, I had fallen in love with her, but I still hadn't mentioned it. Since we lived too far apart to spend time together in person, we resorted to texting and the occasional phone call. Even if nothing more came of it, I was content just staying in touch with her. It was comforting to have someone to share the experience with. Of course, we didn't just reminisce about what had happened—we also kept talking about those letters.

I never returned to the dig site in Mexico. Somehow, digging up prehistoric invertebrates just didn't feel as exciting anymore. I couldn't stop thinking about the subway car, and neither could Shun. We spent a lot of our free time researching different subway systems, trying to find a subway car with a word containing the letters "B," "h," and "z." It was like searching for a needle in a haystack. We had no success, and after a few months, I began to think that the subway car we were looking for hadn't even been built yet. I told myself it was time to move on, but just a few days later, I received a phone call.

"What's your favorite dinosaur?"

"Rodney, is that you?"

"Yes!"

"I'm happy to hear from you. How are you doing?"

"I found it."

"You found it?"

"Yes!"

"A-are you talking about the subway car?"

"Yes!"

"Well, where is it?"

"It's in Stockholm!" Rodney's childish excitement made me smile. "The name of the car is Balthazar. It fits with the letters and the spaces between them. All the subway cars in the Stockholm metro have different names. This one is named after Professor Balthazar from the Croatian animated TV series. It was made for children and focuses on an old inventor. It was produced between sixty-seven and seventy—"

"Okay, slow down," I said, smirking at his typical demeanor. "I don't need all the details about that. Are you saying this subway car is currently being used in the Stockholm metro?"

"Yes, aren't you paying attention?"

As I spoke, I hastily texted Shun: "Talking to Rodney right now. He found it!"

"Rodney, have you told anybody else?" I asked.

"No, it's our secret."

"Okay, good. Where are you now?"

"In Stockholm!"

"What?" I was more than a little surprised. "How did you—"

"First, I took a taxi to Toronto Pearson Airport, and there I bought a ticket to—"

"Right," I interrupted. "Well, have you located the subway car?"

"I'll wait for you and Dr. Chen. I'm staying at the Radisson Blu Waterfront Hotel. And hurry up! I *hate* waiting."

After ending the call, my mind was racing. The prospect of going to Stockholm to investigate the subway car was too extraordinary to pass up. It would be foolish not to pursue it, and equally foolish to leave without uncovering the answers we sought. The only thing that gave me pause was the uncertainty of the timeline. We might find our answers in a day, or it could take years—if we found them at all.

Shun texted me and said that she was already packing, but I still needed some time to think it all over. In the end, however, I decided to take a leave of absence from the university. Shun gave me some additional motivation to go, just by going herself. If I came along, it would mean I would get to meet her again and maybe get a chance to be with her like I had wanted for so long.

I bought a plane ticket to Stockholm and nearly packed my entire wardrobe, unsure of when I'd be back. Part of me wondered if I should've prepared more for the possibility of traveling back in time, but the idea of catching the subway car at the "right" moment—if such a moment even existed—still seemed insane to me. It would likely take years of searching, with no guarantee of success. I was content just going there to see if we could uncover any clues.

Shun arrived a few hours before me and was waiting at Arlanda Airport when I got there. I found her sitting at a café, her many heavy bags gathered close around her. When she spotted me, she broke into a smile, and my excitement grew. Adjusting my hat, I hurried over, pressing through the crowd. She stood up and greeted me with a gentle hug that lasted a bit longer than I expected, yet still left me wanting more. It wasn't something I consciously thought about, just a subtle, unspoken longing. As I sat down, ready to ask how she'd been and what she'd been up to, she spoke first, not giving me the chance.

"Rodney is a genius," she said. "I still can't believe he figured it out. Honestly, I never thought we'd actually find that subway car—even if it was still operational. But somehow, he pulled it off. And traveling all the way to Stockholm by himself? I didn't even know he was capable of doing that."

I laughed. "He explained it to me very matter-of-factly. You know, as long as there's a protocol—or a clear enough set of instructions—I think he's fine. He only struggles when things divert from the expected path. At least, that's how I've come to understand his condition." I paused for a moment, making sure it was safe to change the topic, then continued, "But how about you, how—"

"The car will be here in five minutes," she said, glancing at her phone. "I ordered an Uber to Rodney's hotel. We should probably head outside." She stood up, checked her pockets to make sure everything was there, and grabbed her bags. "By the way, how have you been, Ian?" she asked, tossing her bangs out of her eyes.

"It's been alright," I replied as we walked toward the exit. "I just finished teaching a course on Jurassic plant life. Did I tell you about that? It's a fascinating subject, and the feedback from the students was great, but… nothing feels quite the same since our time in the Yukon."

"I hear you," Shun said as she stepped onto the sidewalk, scanning the area for our car. "Looking at fossils, speculating about what might have been, it all feels different when you know there's an actual link between our present and the past out there, just waiting to be found. I've tried to ignore it—tried living my life like nothing happened—but I can't shake the feeling that I'm settling for less while doing my research, and it's really weighing down on me."

"And now we've found it," I said as we walked up to the car. "The link."

Rodney opened the door to his hotel room with a wide smile, wearing a t-shirt that read "I Love Trains" with a locomotive printed on it. He took a few steps back to let us in, careful not to get too close. As we stepped into the small, one-bed room, Shun asked him how he'd been doing. Placing himself awkwardly in the corner—likely finding the room too crowded with three people and several large bags—he responded with a quick, "Good."

"That's great, Rodney," I said, taking off my hat and ruffling my hair to get rid of the hat's imprint. "Did you take some time to explore the city?"

"No." I waited for him to elaborate, but he didn't say anything more.

Shun, standing by the window and caught in a sunbeam, said, "I think the first question we need to ask ourselves is how to make sure we're on that train the day it goes back in time."

"Time travel," Rodney said dreamily. "This particular subway train travels between—"

"We need to study the subway car as discreetly as possible," I interrupted, "and try to figure out which day it might go back. Right now, we don't even know if it's going to travel back in time at all. It's still possible that one of Miguel's more down-to-earth explanations is true. And even if it does travel back in time, it could be years—maybe even decades—from now. To avoid riding this specific subway car every day, just living on hope, we need to investigate—"

"Ian..." Shun interrupted gently. "We still need to ride it every day. If we can figure out the date, that's great, but until then, we have to assume that any day is just as likely as any other. This expedition could very well take years—"

"We'd have to live like homeless people," I said, "giving up everything for the slim chance—"

"So?" Shun said. "I'm ready to sell my apartment if I have to. This is a once-in-a-lifetime opportunity—to go back in time and witness... I don't need to explain it to you, Ian. Riding a subway every day will be a small price to pay, even if it takes years. I'm trying to see it as one long journey rather than being stuck. People used to jump on ships just to explore, without knowing when—if—they'd ever reach their destination or make it back. They did it on the open sea, facing the wrath of the ocean and the threat of pirates. If we can't do what they did, in one of the safest modes of transportation, in one of the safest countries in the world, what does that say about us?"

I gazed into her eyes, feeling nothing but admiration. "Right," I said. "But still, if we can narrow down the day—"

"You don't need to worry," Rodney interjected, his smile widening. "The Traffic Administration has ordered forty-eight new trains of model C30 at a cost of five billion Swedish crowns. They're being manufactured in Germany, and deliveries have already started. Right now, they're conducting tests without passengers. After that, passenger trials will take place, and the results will be evaluated before the trains become fully operational, likely within one to two years. Initially, these new trains will run exclusively on the Red Line—where Balthazar is currently in use—gradually replacing the older trains."

"That means we have a time frame!" Shun exclaimed. "We know the subway car will travel back in time before it's decommissioned, since there was a passenger inside the remains."

"A maximum of two years, then." I swallowed hard. "We'd basically have to live within the metro system during that time if we can't pinpoint the exact day. How will we support ourselves? And—seriously—how will we even manage basic things like going to the bathroom?"

"They have public restrooms here and there," Shun said. "I wouldn't say that's our biggest hurdle. Supporting ourselves will be the main issue, but again—I'm willing to sell my apartment if I need to."

"We'll figure it out," Rodney said. "It will be fun!"

"Still," I said, "we'll basically be living like the beggars who ride the subway all day."

"But we won't be beggars!" Shun countered. "We'll be on a scientific expedition, albeit an unusual one. And two years is just the worst-case scenario—it isn't that long."

Growing impatient with all our talking, Rodney burst out, "I want to live on this train and go see some dinosaurs. I love trains and dinosaurs."

I didn't think it was responsible to bring Rodney along. He had been a great help to us, but he didn't seem to grasp how dangerous our plans were. If we somehow succeeded with the impossible, I couldn't imagine him surviving for long.

"It's not safe," I said, trying to gently dissuade him from his own determination. "We might not make it, and if we do—if we actually get there—there's no way of knowing if we'll ever return to our own time. And there won't be any other trains there, you know."

"I don't care," he said, rocking back and forth. "I want to go as soon as possible. I can help—trust me, I know a lot about dinosaurs too. While I was waiting for you, I read the entire *Encyclopedia of Dinosaurs* and a bunch of academic articles on the Cretaceous Period."

"There's a lot more to it than just dinosaurs," I said. "It's about surviving in the wild—"

"I'll read about that too."

"You can't learn that solely from a book," I insisted. "It's about experience—"

"He's an adult," Shun said. "Ultimately, it's up to you, Rodney, but please, please, please… understand that it will be extremely challenging. You'll be risking your life, and you may never return. We'll do everything we can to keep you safe if you join us, but I can't stress this enough—it's not going to be like in the movies—"

"I don't watch movies," Rodney said. "I like facts. While you might be switching from a comfortable, predictable environment to one that's uncomfortable and unpredictable, I've always lived in the uncomfortable and unpredictable. I've spent my entire life learning to live with that—constantly and consciously adapting. Maybe I'm more ready than you think. And it's not like I'm leaving anything of value behind. You're my only friends."

Shun gave him a pitying smile. "Okay, well, in that case, let's discuss the practical details of our plan…"

Our first order of business in Stockholm was securing accommodations at the modest but welcoming Bredängs Hostel. Conveniently located near the subway station—our launchpad for tracking Balthazar—the hostel provided us with a simple three-bed room that served as our base camp for sleep and strategy sessions. Luxury wasn't a priority. I had survived far harsher environments in less-developed corners of the world, where cockroaches were common companions, water damage was the norm, and the tap ran brown. Compared to those experiences, this hostel felt like an oasis, complete with clean water and the luxury of heated showers.

As the first light of dawn streaked across the Swedish sky the next morning, we dove into the task of inventorying our gear. The objective was to determine what we could realistically carry with us each day on the subway car. We had the essentials covered: breathable clothing suited for hot climates, rugged waterproof boots, and comprehensive first aid kits stocked with everything from bandages and antiseptic wipes to sunscreen and a variety of over-the-counter remedies. Our utility tools were just as practical, including knives, can openers, and fire starters. In addition, I had packed compasses and star charts for navigation, though their usefulness was questionable given the vast temporal leap to the Late Cretaceous period. Shun, ever diligent in her research, had dedicated an entire bag to documentation and analysis tools—an area I had overlooked, too focused on survival gear.

Despite our extensive array of equipment, our inventory was still missing several crucial items: a sturdy, easy-to-set-up tent, sleeping bags, ropes, water purifiers, fishing gear, walkie-talkies, a compact stove, a supply of nutrient-dense food with utensils, a roll of solar panels, and perhaps most importantly, weapons and ammunition. While most of these items were easily accessible from local stores or online, the last category posed a significant challenge. Firearms, as one might expect, weren't readily available in Sweden. My Canadian hunting license was useless as a mere visitor in this Nordic country.

We considered forgoing firearms, but in the end, the risk seemed too great—or at least, I thought so. Consequently, I dedicated considerable time to finding alternative ways to procure them. I ventured into a neighborhood known for its ties to organized crime, hoping to find someone who could help.

Finally, after striking up a conversation with a group of teens outside a hot dog stand, I connected with a man named Hakim. He wore a black puffer jacket over a branded Adidas hoodie, the logo prominent on his chest. Slim-fit joggers and spotless Nike sneakers completed his outfit. A silver chain glinted from beneath his hoodie, and his neatly cropped hair gave him a polished look. His demeanor wasn't overtly aggressive, but there was something off in the way he eagerly offered to help, making me take a step back.

Nevertheless, I felt cornered—we needed weapons for our defense. Hakim led me to an apartment in a concrete high-rise, one of several identical buildings in a row, each as unremarkable as the next. I felt like I was walking into a trap, but having brought no cash, I figured a robbery was unlikely. The transaction would be conducted using the cryptocurrency Monero, with payments due both before and after receiving the goods. I assumed this meeting was meant to assess my character and clarify exactly what I intended to purchase.

Three men greeted me in the apartment's living room, none of whom shared Hakim's harmless demeanor. Two sat in separate chairs, while the third lounged in the center of a couch, his attention fixed on a football match playing on a massive TV—likely funded by their illicit activities. A baby's cry echoed from a nearby room, oddly comforting amid the tension, and a woman in a hijab quickly rushed to attend to it. Taking a deep breath to steady myself, I stepped further into the room. Hakim remained in the hallway, gesturing for me to go ahead. One of the men, puffing on a joint, burst into laughter when he saw me.

"Who do you think you are?" he jeered. "Crocodile Dundee?"

Surprised by the unexpected reference, I managed a tentative smile. Just then, the man on the couch bellowed at the TV, probably because the wrong team had scored. Tearing his gaze from the match, he met my eyes with a grin.

He stood up, clapped me on the shoulder, and extended a hand, offering me a cigarette and baklava before I could even respond. Hollering something at the woman, he pulled out a chair for me. What followed was a surprisingly cordial discussion, during which the man, in broken but deliberate English, explained how things would proceed. Despite the friendly banter, an unspoken threat lingered in the air—any hint of suspicion or deviation on my part would have serious consequences. I stayed calm and explained candidly what I needed. Ideally, I would've preferred a larger hunting rifle, but the impracticality of carrying one on the subway forced me to settle for smaller automatic firearms—three of them, along with as much ammunition as possible. I also requested a set of hand grenades.

"What do you need all this for?" the man asked, his eyes narrowing. "Planning to invade a country?"

Unable to tell him the truth—that I needed the weapons for a potential time-travel trip to face dinosaurs—I stammered out a hasty lie. "I-I need them for my, uh... survival bunker in the woods."

The man broke into a grin. "Ah, a doomsday prepper, huh? Think the world's ending soon? Well, that'd probably be good for business." He laughed. "Here's the deal: transfer half the money now, we'll deliver the goods, then you send the other half. Sound good?"

I nodded in agreement and fumbled with my phone as I pulled up the digital wallet app that Hakim had mentioned earlier. After a few taps, I scanned the QR code the man provided and sent the cryptocurrency—watching the transaction process gave me an odd sense of unreality. I couldn't help but think about the absurd amount I was spending, far more than I'd ever imagined paying for something like this. Yet, given the circumstances, price seemed a small concern compared to survival.

Hakim, who had quietly lingered in the hallway throughout the entire meeting, stepped forward to escort me out once the transaction was complete. I shook his hand at the entrance, offering a quick nod of thanks before making my way down the concrete stairwell. The tension still weighed on me, and once outside, I broke into a sprint, rushing through the unfamiliar streets and back toward the safety of my hostel.

Rodney had fallen asleep when I returned, but Shun had stayed up waiting for me—clearly worried, which I found endearing. It was a small comfort, a subtle sign that maybe she cared about me just as much as I cared about her.

"How did it go?" she asked, looking up at me from her chair.

I reassured her, explaining that everything had gone smoothly.

She sighed and shook her head. "I really hope those people won't cause any trouble, like tracking you, extorting more money, or just showing up unannounced. And then there's the risk of the police catching wind of this—it would bring our entire expedition to a grinding halt. I know we've discussed it already, and I get why we need weapons for protection, but I can't shake this feeling of anxiety about the whole thing."

"You know I share your concerns," I said, taking off my jacket and hanging my hat on the rack. "But yeah, we need the weapons, and thankfully the hardest part is behind us—now I just have to receive the goods and send the rest of the payment."

"When will that happen?" she asked. "And how?"

I hesitated for a moment before replying, "I'm not entirely sure... they'll send me a message when it's time."

Shun shook her head again, then stood up and walked over to me. She placed a hand on my shoulder, making my heartbeat quicken. "Well, I'm just glad you made it through tonight without any trouble—we can't do this without you. Now, let's get some sleep."

It wasn't long before a notification popped up on Telegram from an unlisted number. The message read: "Meet us behind Leif's Dry Cleaning at 9 PM. Come alone." A cold sweat washed over me as I read the message. Strangely, the thought of actually receiving the weapons made me far more nervous than striking the deal in the first place. Every possible thing that could go wrong flashed through my mind, and an anxious knot tightened in my gut. It was all insane, and a part of me screamed that I should abandon this madness and retreat to the safety of my home in Canada. The thought of dying for this expedition, now more vivid than ever, was almost unbearable. That prospect—the permanent end of consciousness—filled me with dread. Yet, whenever I thought of Shun, of being with her, it stirred something deeper within me, a feeling powerful enough to override my lifelong fear of death. Thus, when the time came, I mustered all my courage, put on my hat, and stepped outside.

The alleyway behind Leif's dry cleaning seemed to swallow the suburb's ambient noise, plunging it into silence. I pulled my jacket tighter against the sharp chill of the Stockholm night. Ahead of me, an imposing figure—not Hakim—emerged from the shadows, his trench coat billowing slightly in the breeze.

"Are you alone?" His gravelly voice cut through the stillness.

I nodded. "Yes."

He gestured toward the trunk of a nondescript sedan. Inside, a duffel bag lay partially open, its contents glinting ominously under the dim glow of a distant streetlamp. My heart thudded against my ribcage.

"We verified the initial payment," he said gruffly. "You'll make the second one now, here, while I watch. Then you take the goods. If you try anything smart, remember—we know who you are and where you live."

Apprehension tightened in my gut as I fumbled with my phone, starting the second cryptocurrency transfer. My fingers trembled slightly as they tapped out the necessary credentials.

Just as I completed the transaction, the back door of Leif's dry cleaning burst open, flooding the alley with light. Leif, presumably, looking thoroughly disgruntled, shouted, "This isn't a marketplace! Take your business elsewhere! I have customers!"

The man by the car shot a venomous look at the man, who, despite his earlier bravado, retreated back into his shop, muttering under his breath.

With the transaction complete, I held up my phone to show the confirmation. The man scrutinized it for a moment, then, satisfied, gestured to the duffel bag.

"Take it and leave. No trouble, understand?"

I nodded and cautiously lifted the bag, its weight a grim reminder of the lethal arsenal inside. Every step I took pulled me further from my previous life, and with the weapons now in my possession, there was no turning back. The expedition had officially begun.

It was early morning when we arrived at Norsborg, the end station on the red line of the Stockholm metro. The elevated platform was bathed in soft spring sunlight, with few people around—most of the concrete suburb still fast asleep.

The train stood waiting to begin its first tour of the day. A peculiar silence hung over the station, as if the world itself was holding its breath. The display showed ten minutes to departure.

We walked along the platform, reading the names on the silver cars. Rodney moved briskly, clearly elated, and when he reached the middle of the platform, he burst into a cheer—he had found Baltazar. We joined him, looking up at the name written in white, italic text.

Standing there in front of the subway car, knowing where it might eventually end up, stirred a peculiar, unsettling feeling. It was as if we were part of a story that had already played out, as though our fates were sealed—or soon would be.

We boarded the train and sat down, our luggage piled between our legs and on the seat next to us. There were twenty-three stations between us and the final stop, and the entire round trip would take about eighty minutes—something we would have to do several times a day, possibly for as long as two years. The thought was dizzying. As departure time approached, more and more passengers began to board the train. A female voice announced something over the speakers in Swedish, words we didn't understand, and then the doors slid shut as the train began to move. A sunbeam caught Shun's face through the window, and she met my gaze. I smiled at her, and she returned the gesture with a brief smile of her own. Rodney, on the other hand, was on full alert, like a child who had just boarded a roller coaster. In truth, that's probably how all three of us felt.

"I'm going to check out the car for a bit," I said. "With a little luck, I might find something that can help us understand what's going to happen—if anything happens at all."

I had no idea what I was looking for, but I hoped I would recognize it when I saw it—maybe some kind of mechanism that didn't belong in a subway car. It seemed reasonable to assume there would be some form of technology on board capable of transporting it back in time.

I walked up and down the aisle, carefully inspecting everything as I went, but nothing unusual caught my eye. To the mild irritation of the passengers, I even crouched down to look under the seats, using the excuse that I thought I had forgotten a bag somewhere in the car. Still, I found nothing of interest there either.

"I didn't find anything that looked out of place," I said as I sat down again. "There should be something in the car that allows it to travel sixty-six million years back in time. Some kind of technology, right? Isn't that a reasonable assumption? Something must have sent it back. It can't just have happened—or it's not just going to happen—randomly, without reason. Maybe it's enough if we examine the car every day and only travel the full distance if we find something unusual. It would save us a lot of time."

"I understand your thinking," Shun said. "But we can't possibly know if we're dealing with something technological or not. It could just as easily be a natural phenomenon of some kind—though I agree, that sounds improbable. And even if technology is involved, we can't be sure whether it's inside the car, outside it, or maybe even hidden somewhere in one of the tunnels."

"That's true," I admitted. "Or maybe this whole thing is a hoax, just like Miguel said, and we'll end up riding this train back and forth for two years for no reason." I laughed at the sheer absurdity of the thought. "But given the evidence we've seen, that seems less likely—fortunately."

By the time we reached Hornstull—fifteen stations into the line—Rodney had opened a book about wilderness survival and was completely absorbed in it, while Shun scrolled through her phone. The car was nearly full now. I glanced at the other passengers, on their way to school or work, and wondered what it would be like to spend the rest of my lives with them, sixty-six million years in the past.

How would the youngest fare? And the oldest? A wave of guilt washed over me for not warning the passengers about what could happen. No one would have believed me, of course—it would probably just end with us being thrown off by the guards—but it still felt wrong to stay silent, as if I was complicit in putting them at risk.

"Are you leaving any important people behind?" I asked as the train turned at Ropsten, the final station.

Rodney looked up from his book, momentarily disoriented. "No. Or..." He paused, thinking. "I'll probably miss trains. But dinosaurs are just as interesting. Plus, now I have you guys. Trains are great, but nothing beats real friends."

"That's very sweet of you to say," I replied, instinctively reaching to pat him on the shoulder before stopping myself, remembering how much he disliked being touched. "And you, Shun?"

"Not really," she said. "I never got along well with my family—that's one of the reasons I moved to Canada instead of staying in China. They wanted me to stay home and help take care of my little sister instead of pursuing my studies. For some reason, my sister got all the attention. They named her Xiuying, which means luxuriant, beautiful, elegant, outstanding. Do you know what my name means? Obey, or submit... That pretty much tells you everything you need to know about my upbringing. I wanted to go my own way."

"I'm sorry to hear that," I said softly. "And now you have no contact with them at all, do you?"

"Hardly," Shun replied, a hint of sadness crossing her face.

"They won't miss me if we end up unable to return to our own time."

"You don't have others you'll miss? Friends or...?" I asked, feeling a pang of worry, as if I was afraid of what her answer might be.

"I've never really taken the time to connect with anyone," Shun admitted. "As a foreigner, it's been difficult to form deeper relationships. Maybe if I'd come to Canada earlier, it would've been easier, but I arrived at twenty-four without knowing anyone. Sure, I got along with my classmates, and later with my colleagues, but none of them would come to my funeral, if you know what I mean. All the traveling for work didn't help either. And you, Ian?"

Relieved that she hadn't mentioned anyone closer to her than a friend, I replied, "It would've been my mom, but she passed away a year ago. My dad disappeared from the picture when I was little, so I have no relationship with him at all. He definitely won't notice if I disappear forever. I've got a couple of close friends I'll miss—and I think, I hope, they'll miss me too—but you can't let those things stop you if you want to write history. Or at least witness it. But yeah, deep down, I hope this isn't a one-way ticket."

"Traveling forward in time should be easier than traveling back," Rodney said. "So, someone who's learned how to travel back in time should reasonably know how to travel forward too."

Back in Norsborg, I desperately needed to use the bathroom, but there was no time. The next trip was agonizing—I had to pace up and down the car just to avoid wetting myself. It wasn't until we reached the final station again, where the train lingered a bit longer before departure, that I finally got the chance to sprint to a public toilet. Not wanting to get separated by mistake, and because Rodney and Shun had the same need, they came with me.

When we returned to the train, only four minutes remained until departure, which meant that if any of us had needed to do a number two, we'd risk missing it. However, this was something we had prepared for. We knew we couldn't possibly ride on every single trip—especially since we needed sleep—but also because we might occasionally miss the train or have to skip a ride for other reasons. The important thing, we had agreed, was to stay together and not get separated.

On the second trip back, we ate the lunch we had prepared the night before—cold lentil stew with rice. We had made enough to last the entire week, hoping to save time by not having to cook during our daily rides.

"This actually doesn't taste so bad," I said, taking another bite. "A few years ago, I was on an excavation in Papua New Guinea, and we stayed with one of the tribes for a few days. They offered us larvae for lunch. We had to accept with polite smiles, but to put it mildly, it wasn't for me. I can eat most things, but insects... that's where I draw the line." I laughed. "I wonder what dinosaur tastes like. I'm not sure I want to find out, though. Hopefully, there are plenty of alternatives where we're going. Just imagine all the fruits and berries that must have existed back then, ones no human has ever tasted. Although, they might not have evolved much flavor—at least, not to our liking."

Shun gave me a warm smile. "We probably won't be able to be too picky," she said. "I think—"

The train jolted. We were somewhere in the tunnel between the Karlaplan and Östermalmstorg stations, a relatively short distance. My heart leapt into my throat. We looked at each other in silence, tense with anticipation. *Was this the moment it would happen?* The train slowed slightly, but then picked up speed again and continued as usual. I exhaled deeply.

"False alarm," Rodney said.

We returned to the hostel at two in the morning, after traveling back and forth between the two end stations about a dozen times. The day had been punctuated by panic-stricken bathroom trips and several false alarms that kept us on edge. I collapsed onto my bed, staring up at the ceiling, already exhausted after just one day.

"It's going to take a while to get used to this life," I admitted, feeling slightly disappointed that nothing had happened, even though we hadn't expected anything this soon.

The next day unfolded much the same, and so did the third, fourth, and fifth. My exhaustion didn't improve; if anything, each day left me more drained than the last. The subway car grew increasingly claustrophobic as time passed. I missed the simple pleasures—breathing fresh air, walking in nature, and being able to use the bathroom whenever I needed. The lentil stew—the quickest and cheapest dish we could cook and therefore the one we were stuck with—didn't taste as good to me anymore as it had on the first day. Soon, I feared I would vomit if I took one bite too many. Meanwhile, Rodney, who had now read several books on survival, spent every morning exercising when the car was nearly empty. It was something he had never done before in his life—his hefty frame made that clear—and I had to assist him with various exercises. However, he learned quickly and continued with his routine every other day, like a robot—following the instructions from one of his survival books to the letter. Personally, I didn't want to exercise publicly in the subway and planned to join a 24-hour gym, hoping to squeeze in an hour or so after our trips. But my exhaustion kept me postponing it. I was already in good shape, but I knew I wouldn't stay that way for long if I didn't get back into training. Shun, on the other hand, often joined Rodney for some of his exercises, though she never completed the entire routine.

By the end of the first week, we decided to skip a day and have a meeting back at the hostel—along with a long-awaited dinner and a bottle of red wine.

"I'm going to sell my apartment," Shun announced as we sat in the hostel's small kitchen. "It should be enough to finance us for at least a year."

I scratched my now unshaven chin. "Are you sure about that? You'll regret it if this doesn't lead anywhere. And don't you have to go back to sell it?"

"It can be arranged from here," she replied. "And if this doesn't pan out, I'll just buy something new. Maybe I'll even take a position at another university—maybe in Australia. I think I'd enjoy it there, in the warmth."

Fear washed over me when she mentioned Australia, but I did my best to hide it. "If we need more money, maybe I should take on some programming jobs? The subway has Wi-Fi. I could work while we ride the train."

"I think we'll need to do both," Shun replied. "That way, we could make things a bit more comfortable—maybe have a slightly more lavish lunch and so on. It's important that we stay as healthy as possible so we're ready for the challenges ahead. Speaking of which, you really need to start training, Ian... Rodney's proven it can be done."

I felt a twinge of shame when she said that. "Yeah," I replied, "it's just a bit awkward doing it on the train. People already think we're a bunch of lunatics. I've been thinking about getting a gym membership. But you're right—I should definitely start training. I might be the one in the best shape right now, but I know that won't last if I don't do something."

Shun turned to Rodney. "Do you have any way to earn money?"

"No," he said, sipping the water he had poured into his wine glass. "But I get social assistance, and I'll probably keep getting it for a while before they notice I'm not in the country."

"Well, that's something," Shun said. "But how do you feel about what we're doing now?"

Rodney looked down at his plate. "You mean the dinner?"

"No," Shun clarified, "I mean everything we're doing—the subway trips and everything around it. Are you still as enthusiastic as before?"

"Oh, yes," Rodney said. "Even more than before. I've found a third interest now—surviving in the wilderness is like a whole science. There's so much to learn! Did you know, for example, you can start a fire with an orange? Citrus oils are flammable. You just make a hole in the top, remove some of the flesh, and let it dry for a bit. Then you put a hard stone inside and rub a knife or stick against it rapidly until a spark strikes the stone."

Shun gave me a teasing look. "Did you know that?"

"No," I said, "but there won't be any oranges where we're going. Though, who knows, maybe we'll find some ancient ancestor of the orange." I laughed. "But seriously, that's great information. However, like I've said before—knowledge is one thing, skills are another. It's important you understand that difference, Rodney. When it's time to actually live in the wilderness, you'll have to learn by doing, and that can be tough. Anyway, we've had this discussion before, so there's probably not much more to say."

A brief silence followed, then Rodney spoke up. "I really don't understand. If you follow the instructions correctly—and if the instructions are right—how can it go wrong?"

A bit frustrated by his mechanical way of thinking, I said,

"There isn't a written instruction for every situation, and even when there are, it often requires mastering unconscious skills like balance, fine motor coordination, and—" I paused when I realized he wasn't following. "Take cycling, for example. No matter how many books you read about it beforehand, you're not going to manage it on the first try."

"In theory, it should be possible to manage it on the first try, but it would require a very long instruction book and a person with an excellent memory." He paused, as if he finally grasped what I was trying to say. "Point taken! I'm really looking forward to converting my knowledge into skills through practice."

"Another thing to remember besides skills and knowledge," I said, "is instinct. In a high-pressure situation—say, being chased by a triceratops—you won't have time or the ability to make logical calculations. You'll have to rely entirely on gut feeling. Those are the moments that will be the most dangerous for you, Rodney. I'm not trying to patronize you, believe me, but I think it's important that you're aware of the challenges ahead, especially the ones that will be tough for you personally."

"I'm not offended," Rodney said with his usual neutral expression. "There's undoubtedly a lot I can improve on, and I appreciate you explaining it to me. However, running from a triceratops would likely be difficult for most people, considering their estimated top speed—thirty-two kilometers per hour—and even those who could keep up wouldn't be able to sustain that pace for long. So, the most sensible thing would be to climb to a height—into a tree or onto a cliff—for shelter. But yes, I understand that was just an example."

"We just want you to understand what you're getting into," I said. "Right, Shun?"

"Absolutely," she agreed. "But I also think it's important we don't underestimate each other."

I wasn't sure why she added that last part. It felt like a subtle criticism, one I didn't think was entirely fair, but I decided not to argue.

The next day, we resumed our routine, traveling with Baltazar and living like underground dwellers. Days turned into weeks, and weeks into months. People began to recognize us, probably assuming we were homeless. Some even gave us coins. My long, scruffy beard probably added to the impression. This became our life: painful, humiliating, and degrading. I eventually bought the gym membership, but I rarely had the energy to use it. And since we weren't eating enough—at least I wasn't, having grown tired of our meager meals—I lost a lot of weight. Eventually, I could hardly recognize myself when I looked in the mirror. Shun had also lost some weight, though not as much as I had. She looked pale, probably from our lack of sleep, but in my eyes, she was as beautiful as ever. The only thing keeping us going was the explorer's dream—to go where no one had gone before and see what no one had seen before. Yet, I could feel reality starting to nibble away at the edges of that dream.

After one year—and a long winter spent without seeing the sun for months—Shun developed a mild depression. I felt the same, though I didn't admit it. Someone had to appear strong, or so I reasoned. It wasn't that she was giving up, it was just the sheer difficulty of the life we were leading. She often cried at night. I tried to comfort her, either by listening or suggesting solutions, but for some reason, it always felt awkward. It was as if there was an invisible wall between us, keeping me—maybe everyone—at arm's length from her. The only thing that seemed to help Shun was fully committing to Rodney's obsessive exercise routine. I tried to join in—now much weaker than when we first started—but I still couldn't find the motivation. Besides, as soon as we got on the train, I usually had to dive into the programming gigs I had taken on, leaving little time for anything else.

Unlike Shun and me, Rodney didn't seem too bothered by our way of life. As long as he could keep reading and studying, he was content. By now, he was more or less an expert in bushcraft and wilderness survival—though only in theory. I admired his ability to retreat into his own little world, where the outside world seemed irrelevant, but I couldn't help worrying about him. Although, after all this time without anything happening, I had begun to doubt that anything would happen at all, in which case we would soon be home and safe again. A part of me—and not a small part—was looking forward to that. Still, I could see the lingering enthusiasm in Shun's eyes, and that alone kept me from giving up. I didn't see it as often as before, though.

Just as Shun was on the verge of giving up under the pressure, six more months into our journey, I spotted a woman on the train who looked oddly familiar. There had been delays—surprisingly common in the Stockholm metro—and the subway cars were packed with people heading home from work. We had given up our seats to a group of elderly women and were standing shoulder to shoulder in the crowd. I couldn't quite place where I'd seen the woman before. Her face kept disappearing behind a group of young men, preventing me from getting a good enough look. That's when Rodney blurted out, "Kira?"

As soon as I heard Rodney say her name, it clicked—I realized it was her. Kira. My immediate assumption was that she had come to arrest us after tracking down our whereabouts. It wouldn't have been hard for them to put two and two together. Or maybe they'd known all along and had simply used us to find the subway car and solve their mystery for them—though

I couldn't figure out why they would've waited until now if that were the case. Either way, seeing her likely meant the end of our expedition and the start of a prison sentence—and not just because of the illegal weapons we were carrying in our bags.

"Step aside!" Kira yelled at the crowd, pulling a gun and pointing it directly at me. Chaos erupted as people screamed and scrambled away from her, creating a clear path between us. My heart raced as I met her gaze.

"Dr. Foster, get over here right—"

I remember the next moment as if it happened in slow motion. The train shook violently, as though it were derailing, yet it kept moving. The lights in the ceiling flickered, plunging us in and out of darkness. Passengers screamed again, some tumbling over each other in the chaos. A strange noise, rising in intensity, echoed all around us. It was clear—the day we had been waiting for had arrived. Nothing else could explain what was happening. I felt a faint electrical sensation crawl across my skin and tasted blood in my mouth. I felt sorry for the passengers, especially the group of children huddled near the doors. They hadn't asked to be part of this. The lights went out completely, and panic spread like wildfire through the trembling carriage. People trampled over each other in the chaos. Here and there, phones lit up, illuminating terrified faces, while somewhere in the darkness, a dog barked frantically. I grabbed Shun's hand, pulling her close just before she was swallowed by the screaming crowd.

"It's happening!" I heard Rodney yell. "It's happening!"

A deafening bang echoed through the carriage. At first, I thought Kira's gun had gone off, but the sound was far too loud. Several windows shattered, sending glass spraying inward, and a woman holding an infant was shoved so violently that she dropped the screaming child into the black void beyond the train. She let out a desperate scream before being thrown backward by another violent jolt. The noise was now so overpowering that the passengers' cries were almost drowned out, and my skin felt like it was on fire. If things got any worse, I thought, we wouldn't survive the journey.

The next second, another bang echoed, and then—instantly—the darkness that had swallowed the little child vanished, replaced by the blinding white light of the sun. Aside from the ringing in my ears and the sound of passengers sobbing, everything became eerily quiet and still. As my eyes adjusted to the brightness, colors and shapes began to form outside the windows. Shun clung to my arm, and the warmth of her touch spread to my chest, grounding me in the overwhelming moment.

"Look how beautiful!" she exclaimed. "We made it—after all this time, we made it!"

Those who had fallen began to get up. I helped one of the older women to her feet; like me, she had a streak of blood under her nose. She sat down in one of the seats, dazed. The woman who had lost her child was crying hysterically, beyond the reach of any comfort. The confusion in the car was too overwhelming for anyone to react. I couldn't help but wonder where her child had gone—whether it was floating endlessly in that darkness or somehow reappearing elsewhere in spacetime.

Slowly, the sobbing gave way to an uneasy murmur. I looked around, searching for Kira. Someone was helping her up from the floor, where she had been pinned beneath an overweight man. Her panic was different from everyone else's, as though she were expecting something far worse to happen. Still dazed, she snatched her pistol from the ground and began pushing through the crowd, frantic to get away from the windows. But the disoriented passengers blocked her path. Then, in that chaotic moment, her eyes locked with mine.

"Dr. Foster!" she shouted. "You have to—"

Her voice was drowned out by the heart-wrenching wails of the mother, whose grief had reached a breaking point. Tears welled up in Kira's eyes as she slowly turned toward the window. She raised the pistol to her temple but couldn't bring herself to pull the trigger. Someone screamed, and the sound cascaded through the crowd like falling dominoes.

In the next moment, my childhood dream came true.

"It's blue!" Rodney exclaimed. "It's blue!"

A massive, scaly head—belonging to a Tyrannosaurus rex—thrust through the shattered window. Its snout was covered in fine, bristle-like feathers, not as thick as imagined but enough to give it a patchy, downy texture. The bluish hue Rodney had noticed likely came from an iridescent sheen that refracted in the sunlight. Its powerful jaws, lined with jagged teeth, clamped around Kira and, with one violent motion, ripped her from the car, vanishing back outside with its prize.

Everyone scrambled away from the window in blind panic. A young girl—maybe just fifteen—fell to the ground, crying out. Trampled in the chaos, her cries gradually faded into silence. One of the elderly women was pressed so hard against the wall that she coughed up blood. In desperation, people began leaping out of the windows on the opposite side of the subway car, trying to escape. But after running just a few meters, they froze in terror at something ahead and came rushing back toward the train car.

I started to feel unsteady, almost dizzy. It didn't take long to realize that the high oxygen levels of this time period were affecting me. I wasn't the only one; another one of the elderly women fainted right in front of me. It was going to take some time to adjust to the atmosphere.

"Please!" Shun yelled to the crowd. "Duck and cover!"

But no one listened. The subway car jolted violently—the Tyrannosaurus rex was back. And it wasn't alone. They circled us, pushing the subway car as if investigating its structure. My terror was mixed with awe. They were majestic, far more imposing than I had ever imagined.

One of the Tyrannosaurs stopped abruptly, tilting its head in a bird-like manner. It let out a loud sound—not a roar, but more of a hoarse grunt. The others paused too, and then, as if spooked, they all took off in a hurry. The subway car filled with the sounds of people screaming and crying, confusion spreading as everyone tried to make sense of what was happening.

I rushed to the window to get a clearer look outside. We were in the middle of what looked like a vast valley, surrounded by dense, ancient forests.

"We're back in Canada," Shun said beside me. "Or, you know, in what will become Canada."

"Somewhere in the north of the supercontinent Laurasia," I said, still catching my breath. "Why did they run off like that?"

"No idea," Shun replied. "But look—what is that?"

She pointed toward a mysterious mountain on the horizon. It was pitch black, standing in stark contrast to the surrounding peaks. Dark spires jutted up around it, and huge clusters of what I could only assume were some kind of pterosaurs circled ominously near the top.

"I don't know—" I began, but before I could say anything else, a tremor rippled through the ground, feeling like a small earthquake.

"Herregud!" someone shouted in Swedish—a language I had become fairly proficient in during our journeys with Baltazar. "Vad i helvete är det där? Vad händer!"

Panic erupted again. I pushed my way to the other side of the subway car and peered out the window. Kira's body lay crumpled on the ground, her head missing. But that wasn't what had terrified everyone.

Something was emerging from the forest. Thousands upon thousands of predatory dinosaurs were sprinting toward us, their sheer numbers shaking the ground beneath them. Shun pushed her way through the panicked crowd trying to flee the subway car and joined me at the window.

"Are they Velociraptors?" she asked.

"They shouldn't be here," I said, my mind racing. "They lived ten million years earlier, and not in this part of the world."

"They look wrong too," Shun said, her eyes narrowing as she studied them.

"Don't just stand there!" someone yelled at us. "We need to get the fuck out of here!"

I ignored the shout, too fixated on the approaching creatures. "They're too white," I said. "It looks like their feathers have been plucked. And what are those black patches all over their bodies? I can't make it out—it looks like some kind of goo. And why are they moving like a herd?"

The dinosaurs were closing in at an alarming speed. Almost all the passengers had climbed out the other side of the subway car, sprinting for their lives, but we stayed. Without even needing to discuss it, we agreed the inside of the car was still the safest place to be.

"They aren't moving like a herd," Shun said. "They're moving like a swarm."

The strangest part was that among the predatory dinosaurs, there were others as well. I spotted several Triceratops—common for this era—and a few Stegosauri, which should have gone extinct millions of years earlier. They were all just as pale, nearly devoid of any pigment except for that odd black substance.

"They're so pale," I said. "They almost look dead."

"This is insane," Shun whispered, panic creeping into her voice. "What the hell is going on here?"

"We won't figure this out now," I said urgently. "They'll be on us in minutes. I think we should climb onto the roof. Do you think we can manage that?"

We left our bags behind in the subway car and helped each other up to the roof as the swarm of dinosaurs drew closer. I climbed up first, then reached down to help Shun. She called for Rodney to come out while I pulled her up. Rodney clumsily tumbled through one of the windows, his eyes darting nervously between the approaching dinosaurs and us.

"Come on Rodney!" Shun yelled. "Take my hand!"

He ran up to us and stared at Shun's hand with more panic than when he had seen the approaching dinosaurs.

"I don't like being touched!" he said.

"You can do it, Rodney!" Shun said. "Trust me."

Only seconds remained now. As the dinosaurs approached, I could see black, crystal-like spikes growing on their heads and bodies. Nothing about these dinosaurs—these creatures—made sense. Rodney scratched his chin frantically, spun around in some kind of frustration, and mumbled something we couldn't hear.

"He can't do it," I said. "He's going to die."

"Rodney!" Shun shouted. "You have to take my hand now if you want to live!"

The first Velociraptor shot past the subway car at an incredible speed, but the second one had its eyes locked on Rodney. Its large, drooling mouth, filled with razor-sharp teeth, almost seemed to form a sinister smile. Rodney squeezed his eyes shut and screamed, then, at the last possible moment, he reached for Shun's hand.

She grabbed his hand and stood up, trying to pull him onto

the roof, but he was too heavy for her. I reached for Shun's hands to help, thinking it was too late. Rodney was only halfway up when the Velociraptor leaped, jaws snapping at his leg. I threw myself backward, pulling Shun with me, and in turn, dragging Rodney up onto the roof—just a fraction of a second before he would have been trapped in the jaws of the beast.

The subway car rocked violently, nearly tipping over as the swarm thundered past. I crawled to the edge, desperate to see where they were heading. In the distance, I could still make out the people fleeing, their panic evident in every frantic movement. I couldn't even begin to imagine how confused they must have been. They had just reached the edge of the forest, but it wouldn't be enough. The swarm was too fast. Dust billowed into the air around us, thick and suffocating, making it even harder to breathe.

We stayed on the roof until everything grew still. The swarm had disappeared into the forest, likely catching up with the fleeing passengers.

"How did Kira know?" I asked, still trying to process what had just happened.

"You think she knew this was the day?" Shun replied.

"Maybe they found some additional clues," I speculated. "But if they knew all along, I'm not sure why she'd come alone."

We couldn't make sense of it. Everything was silent now, an unsettling calm after the chaos. Slowly, we stood up, taking in our surroundings for the first time without distractions. The forest-covered hills around us sparkled like emeralds in the sunlight.

"It looks so young," I said. "The Earth looks young."

"Actually," Rodney said, still catching his breath, "Earth is still billions of years—"

"I know," I interrupted, "but can't you feel it? A world without humans, without civilization. Right now, we are the most intelligent beings on the planet!"

As I spoke, my eyes drifted toward the ominous black mountain on the horizon. The organic-looking spires swayed slightly in the wind, adding an unsettling, alien quality to the landscape.

"Everyone ran into the forest to seek shelter," Shun said, looking in the opposite direction. "Do they even stand a chance?"

"Look around you," I said, gesturing to the mutilated bodies scattered around us, left behind by the swarm. "I can't imagine anyone got very far."

"Some of them might have managed to climb a tree," Rodney said. "But I agree, it doesn't look good. Still, it might be a good idea to investigate—"

"No," I cut in. "It's too dangerous. Even with our weapons, we wouldn't stand a chance. We can't risk our lives like that—not with odds like these."

"Agreed," Shun said. "We need to move to a safer location, pronto—get our bearings straight. Only then can we even consider if there were any survivors. Though, I doubt it..." She sighed. "What a tragic mess."

"It's not our fault," I replied. "No one would've believed us until it was too late."

"What are we going to do about the bodies?" Shun asked, pointing at Kira and the other victims. "Should we come back to bury them?"

"If it's safe enough," I said. "But right now, we need to focus on finding somewhere to set up camp."

"It'll probably never be safe enough down here," Shun said, her words heavy with sadness. "Poor Kira. She was a good person. Are you sure we're not to blame?"

"No," I replied firmly. "Kira knew what she was getting into."

We climbed down from the subway car and grabbed our

bags. I wasn't used to holding a submachine gun—but when I pulled it out, it gave me an unexpected sense of confidence I never would've had otherwise in a place like this. Shun retrieved her gun too, her expression steely as she checked the weapon.

"Stick close to us, Rodney," she said. "Don't wander off."

"We need to take advantage of our mammalian flexibility," I said. "Our best bet is either up in the trees or in the hills."

"The hills," Rodney said. "We need a cave!"

"He's right," Shun agreed. "We can't risk making a fire out in the open. With these high oxygen levels, even wet plants could catch fire."

We headed toward the largest hill. I paused for a moment to look back at the subway car. Seeing it standing in the middle of this valley at the end of the Cretaceous Period felt surreal. How had it ended up here? So far, none of our questions had been answered; instead, more had arisen.

As soon as we stepped into the forest at the foot of the hill, we heard the rustling of smaller animals—perhaps even our own prehistoric cousins—skittering away through the underbrush. An awful stench hung in the air, growing stronger as we continued. Small avian creatures—possibly Rahonavis, judging by their raised sickle claws—flew toward the source of the smell. When we finally reached it, we saw it came from the rotting carcass of a recently deceased Alamosaurus.

It was gigantic, easily thirty meters from its long tail to its neck. Small, feathered creatures—likely avian dinosaurs—circled the massive corpse, while insects and arthropods swarmed over it in a frenzy. Just seeing the bugs made my sweaty skin crawl.

"Are you okay?" Rodney asked, smiling as if he hadn't realized the danger we were in. "You look pale."

"I—I'm okay," I said, wiping my forehead. "It's just so freaking humid here."

"Look at those," Shun said, pointing at a large group of centipedes crawling in and out of the corpse. "They're white, just like the strange dinosaurs in the swarm. And—yes—there's something black on them as well. Do you think—"

"That black stuff," I interrupted. "Yeah, it's the same. It looks like some kind of parasitic fungus. Could that be what's affecting them?"

"It doesn't explain the lack of pigment, but yes," Shun replied, her brow furrowed.

Something large moved through the forest nearby, startling us.

"Let's move on," I said, glancing nervously at the carcass. "This thing is going to attract larger predators sooner or later, and I don't want to be here when they show up."

As we continued deeper into the forest, climbing the hill, our conversation turned back to the mysterious black substance.

"I have a crazy idea," Shun said.

"Well," I replied, "given what we've been through, I don't think crazy and unbelievable mean the same thing anymore."

"I'm sure you're familiar with it already," Shun said. "There's a fungus in the tropics—an insect-pathogenic fungus. I can't remember its name right now, but it basically takes control of its hosts. It infects ants. You've heard about it?"

"Ophiocordyceps unilateralis!" Rodney blurted out, still gazing around in awe at everything. His voice took on a factual tone, almost as if he were reciting from an encyclopedia: "Infected hosts leave their nests in the trees and descend to the forest floor, where the temperature and humidity are optimal for fungal growth."

"I think I've read about it somewhere," I said.

"The infected ants use their mandibles to attach themselves to a major vein on the underside of a leaf," Rodney continued, still sounding like a walking encyclopedia, "and they remain there after death."

"What if this fungus—if that's what it is—is some prehistoric relative of that species?" Shun said. "Taking control of its hosts. That could explain the behavior we saw earlier."

"I don't know," I replied, shaking my head. "That still doesn't explain the anachronisms—the dinosaurs that should've been extinct. There was a freaking Stegosaurus among them. And again, why didn't they have any pigments?"

"The lack of pigment could be a symptom," Shun suggested. "But yeah, you're right. Dinosaurs from the past, mammals from the future... None of it adds up."

Larger animals—like the Tyrannosaurus rex—wouldn't be good climbers, so we chose the steepest part of the hill to minimize the risk of becoming their next meal. As we ascended, the trees grew sparser, which helped with the oppressive humidity but exposed us to the scorching sun. We paused for a moment, sitting against a cliff, and drank from the water we'd brought with us. The view over the valley was breathtaking. In the distance, we could still see the subway car, now far away. Its remaining windows reflected the sunlight, giving it an out-of-place glow in this ancient world.

"Something's moving down there," Shun said, rummaging through her bag for her binoculars. "Can you see it?"

I squinted, spotting two large figures near the subway car.

"Quetzalcoatlus," Shun breathed, peering through the binoculars. "My God, there's two of them!"

They were the largest known flying animals to have ever lived. Excitement surged through me as I quickly dug out my own binoculars, eager to see them up close. But the moment I laid eyes on them, a sinking dread mingled with my excitement.

They were both unnaturally white, their bodies coated in the same black substance we had seen before. One of them had its head inside the subway car, dragging out one of the dead passengers. It gripped the body in its massive, sharp beak. The other one picked up Kira's lifeless body with an almost casual ease.

"What are they doing?" I asked, unable to tear my eyes away.

The two Quetzalcoatlus spread their massive wings—stretching more than ten meters across—and took off with the bodies still clutched in their beaks.

"They're flying toward the black mountain," Shun said.

"What do you think it is?" I asked, following their path.

"Some kind of nest?" Shun suggested, though she sounded uncertain.

We watched in silence as the Quetzalcoatlus soared through the sky, eventually merging with the other dots circling the black mountain.

"We need to get moving, find someplace to set up camp," I said, standing up and continuing our climb.

Out of nowhere, Rodney spoke. "You were wrong."

"About what?" I asked, tossing my bag onto a ledge and pulling myself up after it. My head still spun whenever I exerted myself, and the ache in my body lingered.

"There's another intelligence here," Rodney said, his voice unsettlingly calm.

"I was thinking the same," Shun said. "From what we've seen so far, we can assume that this fungus—or whatever it is—has some form of swarm intelligence. The way those dinosaurs moved in unison, and now the Quetzalcoatlus collecting bodies for the rest of the swarm."

"Physarum polycephalum," Rodney said.

"What's that?" I asked, confused.

"It's my favorite slime mold," he replied. "What's yours?"

"I don't really have a favorite slime mold, Rodney," I said, suppressing a smile. "Is there something special about it that makes you bring it up now?"

"Yes," he replied simply.

I reached out to help him up the cliff, but as always, he refused to be touched, opting instead to climb up on his own. Unsurprisingly, after all his recent exercise, he managed it with ease.

"Well, what is it?" I asked once he stood next to me.

"As I said, it's a slime mold," Rodney replied. "It doesn't have a nervous system, but it still shows signs of intelligent behavior. It can navigate mazes, store nutrients efficiently, avoid traps, and even balance its nutritional intake."

"I've read about that," Shun said as she reached the top of the hill a few meters above us. "Maybe this is some kind of advanced version of that species. The real question is: how smart is it?"

"It's an animal, so I still think I was right in saying we're the most intelligent beings—" I began, but Shun cut me off.

"I think we should set up camp here," she said, surveying the area. "It's unlikely a larger predator could reach the top of this hill, and it's a bit less humid. The only problem is fire. One stray spark could set the entire forest—and us—ablaze."

"Maybe we can build an oven," I suggested, "using some rocks or, ideally, clay if we can find any."

"That's a good idea," Shun agreed. "I'm just concerned about the smoke. It'll draw attention."

"You really think it's that intelligent?" I asked again, still doubting. "You think it could actually recognize a stream of smoke as a sign of our presence?"

"We've been mysteriously brought back in time," Shun replied. "We can't take any chances here."

"Without fire, we won't survive for long," I said, pressing my point. "I say we take the risk."

With that, we began setting up the tents. We had brought two compact but surprisingly spacious ones: a larger, four-person tent for communal living and a smaller, two- to three-person tent meant to house the portable research equipment we'd need to study and document the Cretaceous environment. As I crouched down to stake one of the tent poles, my hand brushed through the grass growing around me. I couldn't help but think about how evolutionarily young it still was during this time period—barely beginning its dominance in Earth's plant life.

Then I noticed something much older—a small insect reminiscent of an earwig. It startled me as it took flight from the top of a blade of grass, buzzing directly toward my face. I flinched, but it veered off harmlessly. It wasn't much larger than the earwigs back home, which didn't surprise me. Thankfully, insects had their heyday during the Carboniferous and Permian periods—more than two hundred million years earlier. However, the largest ant to have ever lived—Titanomyrma gigantea, ants as large as hummingbirds—wouldn't emerge until the Eocene, ten million years into the future from our current perspective. Hence, the possibility of encountering insects larger than what we were accustomed to remained a minor concern. My desire to witness living creatures from this period of Earth's history had its limits, and it stopped firmly at oversized arthropods.

After we finished setting up the larger tent, I stood up, nearly fainting from a sudden drop in blood pressure, and walked over to the bag with the smaller tent alongside Shun. A few meters away, Rodney was busy unfurling the solar panels, connecting them to our electronics—walkie-talkies, a drone, laptops, and a few scientific instruments.

"Be careful with that microscope!" Shun called out as we pulled the smaller tent from the bag. "It's fragile!"

"I know!" Rodney responded with a nervous smile, nodding as he handled the equipment gingerly.

A faint headache began creeping in, most likely from the relentless heat and the oxygen-rich atmosphere. "It's going to take some time to adjust to these atmospheric conditions, right?" I said, rubbing my temples.

"I felt a bit lightheaded on our way up," Shun replied, "but I'm better now. Are you still feeling it?"

"Not much," I said, downplaying it. "Just a small headache and some dizziness."

Shun began unfolding the tent. "You should get some rest. Rodney and I can handle the rest."

"Out of the question." I took the tent poles from her hand with a grin. "I'm not going to sit around doing nothing while you two do all the work."

"We need you at full capacity." Shun gave me a look, like a disapproving parent. "Don't push yourself just out of pride."

"Look," I said, "if it gets any worse, I'll take a nap—promise! But I can handle a small headache."

We proceeded to stake down the second tent, after which Shun began organizing the scientific equipment inside. I walked over to the bag containing our weapons and double-checked that everything was accounted for. I pulled out the FN SCAR-L rifle left inside and the H&K 416, along with the grenades and ammunition. These were our last resort, meant only for life-or-death situations, but they needed to be accessible at all times. I made sure to load each gun, then placed them near the entrance of the larger tent. Eventually, I thought, I'd build a more secure storage solution for them.

"Listen," I said, "I just loaded the guns and placed them

near the entrance in case of emergencies—just so you're both aware. Once you're ready, let's secure the perimeter around the campsite."

While I waited for them, I prepared the tools we had brought for this purpose: a spool of nearly invisible nylon wire, a few metallic bells, and some canisters meant to be filled with pebbles as makeshift alarms. The contrasting sounds these objects would make when disturbed would not only alert us to any intrusions but also help us pinpoint where the threat was coming from. A melodic jingle would indicate something approaching from the east, while a coarse rattling would signal danger from the west—depending on where along the wire we hung the different items. This simple yet ingenious system would give us some peace of mind, though it wouldn't offer much protection against pterosaurs attacking from above or smaller creatures like venomous spiders, scorpions, and snakes. What really made me nervous, however, were the prehistoric insects—wasps, bees, ants, mosquitoes, ticks, and likely many other kinds unknown to man—that could sting or bite. The thought of those creatures lurking nearby was enough to keep me on edge. Hence, we would always have to stay on our guard, no matter what.

Rodney stayed behind, ensuring the drone was fully operational—a key tool for mapping the larger area around our campsite—while Shun and I began setting up the trip wire. The wire allowed us to enclose an area of around 150 meters, but the sparse terrain on the summit limited us to about 80 meters. Still, it was enough to provide sufficient space for our tents, equipment, and ourselves. I even thought there might be room for a makeshift gym—something I had sorely missed during our time traveling in the Stockholm metro.

As Shun hung the bells, I focused on filling the canisters. Eyes scanning the ground for pebbles of the right size, I noticed another one of those earwig-like insects. Moments later, I spotted a third one and before I knew it, they were everywhere around me. It dawned on me that they might be eusocial—and sure enough, shortly after, I stumbled upon their nest near a dead tree. The structure resembled a hybrid between an anthill and a beehive, an enclosed, cone-shaped dome. I swallowed hard as I watched the creatures—some winged, some not—crawl around the nest in the thousands, if not millions.

Looking down again, I let out a yell I'm not proud of when I saw several of them crawling up my pants. I dropped the canister and frantically brushed at my legs, my heart pounding in my chest. Grabbing the canister again, I bolted away, still swatting at the bugs clinging to me.

Shun appeared in front of me, holding one of the guns. "Are you okay? What happened?"

"I'm okay," I blurted out. "That won't help against this problem." I pointed at the gun, only to notice one of the earwigs latched onto my finger. Panic gripped me again as I let out another scream, violently shaking my hand to dislodge it. That's when I felt it—an excruciating pain searing through my finger, traveling up my nerves until it burned through my cheeks. "The son of a bitch bit me!"

"What bit you? Ian, try to focus! What bit you?" Shun's voice was sharp, trying to cut through my panic.

The insect was long gone, but I kept shaking my hand, naively hoping it would rid me of the pulsating pain.

"It feels like I'm on fire," I said, stumbling toward the tents. "Quick, hand me the first aid kit!" As much as the venom itself, I feared an allergic reaction. "Holy shit, it hurts."

Rodney joined us, confusion written all over his face. "What happened to you, Ian?"

Frantically searching for the EpiPen, I gasped, "Some kind of insect bit me—looked like an earwig, but with wings." The pain was too intense for me to keep rifling through the first aid kit. It was the worst pain I'd felt since my kidney stone ordeal a decade earlier. I collapsed onto my side, clutching my hand and struggling to breathe. "There's a whole nest... swarming with these things... right outside the perimeter," I managed between groans.

Both Shun and Rodney crouched beside me. "It doesn't look like you're having an allergic reaction," Shun said, handing me a pill. "Here, take this—it's a strong ibuprofen."

I let her press it between my trembling lips, and Rodney promptly poured water into my mouth. "If it's just pain," Rodney said, "the venom's main function is likely to incapacitate. Uncomfortable, yes, but it shouldn't cause any lasting harm, unless you've got some pre-existing condition."

"It feels like I'm going to die!" I wailed.

"That's highly unlikely," Rodney replied, his voice flat as ever. "We're sixty-six million years in the past, and humans haven't evolved yet. These prehistoric insects may be unfamiliar, but it's improbable that their venom is lethal to us—humans weren't part of their ecosystem."

"Since when did you become a doctor?" I asked, frustrated by his calm, clinical tone. "This is a nightmare!"

"I read it in *Prehistoric Life: A Definitive Visual History of Life on Earth*," Rodney explained. "It has a chapter dedicated to prehistoric insects and their interactions with other species. It doesn't specifically talk about humans, since we weren't around, but it gives a general understanding of how venom evolved."

"Great," I moaned, clutching my throbbing hand.

"Let's get him inside the tent," Shun said, glancing down at me with concern. "We'll monitor your condition, but you've got to stay calm. Panic can make the pain seem even worse."

With that, they carefully lifted me up, and we headed for

the tent. Inside of it, I tossed and turned, barely aware of time passing as I heard Shun and Rodney murmuring outside. After what felt like hours, Shun's head appeared through the tent flap.

"How are you feeling now? Here, take some water, but don't drink too much—we haven't found a reliable water source yet." She handed me one of the bottles we'd packed.

"Can—" My voice came out weak and raspy. "Can you stay with me for a while?"

"We need to finish securing the perimeter before the sun sets," she said gently. "The trip wire has to be up before dark. I promise I'll be back as soon as we're done."

"Be careful," I whispered. "I'm sorry I'm not of more help."

"Don't worry," she said with a reassuring smile. "We've got this. Now just rest, okay?"

Time kept blurring as I lay there—I couldn't tell if minutes or hours passed before the pain finally started to fade. Even though the worst of it was over, I stayed on the sleeping mat, struggling to calm down. My mind was on edge, always imagining one of those cursed bugs sneaking into the tent. However much I tried, I couldn't let my guard down.

The sound of the tent's zipper being pulled open made my heart race. I hoped it was Shun, but when I looked up, my eyes landed on Rodney. "How are you holding up?" he asked, his gaze skimming over everything in the tent but avoiding me directly for some odd reason.

"I'm down here," I said, waving weakly at him. "Where's Shun?"

"She's outside." He paused, then, seemingly realizing he should offer more detail, added, "…doing some work."

"We need to remove that nest," I said, shifting uncomfortably. "This hilltop is too small for both of us."

"I agree," Rodney replied. "But we should wait until after sunset."

"How about we do it right away?" I suggested. "Won't it be too dark after sunset?"

"That would be unwise, Ian," he said calmly.

"Why?" I asked, feeling slightly irritated that I had to pry for an explanation. "Why would it be unwise?"

"Insects are usually calmer at night," Rodney explained, still avoiding eye contact. "If we try now, we risk aggravating them. It's safer to handle them when they're less active."

"If we throw one of our grenades at them, I bet it wouldn't matter." I smiled slyly. "Those fuckers wouldn't see it coming."

Rodney stared at me with his usual blank expression. "That would be extremely reckless."

"I know," I said, shaking my head. "I wasn't serious… Jesus, Rodney. I just want them gone, you know?"

"Ah," he said with a small nod, "I can understand that. I'm sure we'll find a safe and swift way to remove them."

I stayed inside the tent, trying to regain my strength, though the constant fear of another insect bite gnawed at me. As dusk fell, I watched the shadows stretch and shift across the tent, the vibrant orange hues fading into somber shades of purple. Outside, I could hear Shun and Rodney talking, their voices carrying softly in the evening air. I couldn't make out the words, but from the tone in Shun's voice, it sounded like the sunset was breathtaking.

I felt a bit down about missing the sunset, but I consoled myself with the thought that it wouldn't be our last in this prehistoric era. As darkness settled, the sounds around us morphed into a chilling symphony of chirping, croaking, squeaking, hissing, and the occasional growl from the hillside below. Steeling myself, I finally stepped outside, making sure to tuck my socks over my trouser legs to ward off any crawling intruders. I was determined to face my newfound enemy head-on.

"Let's kill some bugs," I said, slipping on my hat as I emerged from the tent. "I can't wait to toss that nest right off the cliff."

Shun, leaning on a spade she'd been using to dig a hole in the middle of the campsite, raised an eyebrow. "We need to assess the situation first. What's the size of the nest, for example?"

I walked over to where she stood, peering into the hole. "It's as big as an anthill," I replied. "What's this for?"

"It's for the fireplace," she said. "I'm planning a Dakota Fire Hole. We can talk more about it tomorrow, but I figured it'd be smart to get a head start."

"That's smart thinking," I said. "Rodney thinks the bugs might be more docile at night, but aside from that, we don't know much about these insects, other than their ability to inflict serious pain. So, how should we proceed?"

Rodney stepped forward, handing out mosquito nets. "We need to cover our faces with these," he said. "I also suggest we wear several layers of clothing, along with gloves and boots. Since we haven't made a fire yet—and probably shouldn't, given the earlier concerns—we can't use smoke to encourage the insects to abandon their nest temporarily. That would've been the ideal solution."

"Right," I said. "The nest is close to the edge of the cliff. What if we use a large branch to push it down the hillside? The fall would shatter it into pieces."

"That might work," Shun said, "but it could backfire if anything goes wrong. Plus, even if we destroy the nest, they might just come back and build another. A better approach might be to cover the entire nest with one of our bags—ensuring there are no openings—and then leave it sealed until morning. At daybreak, we can carefully transport the bag down the slope and release them at a safe distance. This way, we deter them from returning and avoid harming the colony."

"Taking a trip outside the campsite just to avoid harming a bunch of bugs doesn't sit well with me," I said. "I can't say I feel much empathy for these creatures, and I doubt you would either if one of them had bitten you. But I do like the bag idea. Once we've got them trapped, we can either tilt a boulder on top or wrap another plastic bag around it to suffocate them. What do you think, Rodney?"

"I prefer living beings over dead ones," Rodney said, "but I agree, a non-essential trip through the forest—especially before we've had time to map out the terrain—would be foolhardy."

Shun stayed quiet for a moment, weighing our options. Then, with a thoughtful look, she said, "We might have a way to handle this without causing unnecessary harm. We could use carbon dioxide."

"Carbon dioxide?" I asked. "How?"

"Well," Shun began, "we brought CO_2 canisters for emergency fire suppression, right? It's non-toxic, odorless, and colorless. Plus, it's heavier than air. If we carefully introduce it into the bag, it will displace the oxygen. The insects would essentially suffocate in their sleep, without suffering."

"That could work," Rodney said. "I almost died from carbon dioxide poisoning once while building a huge train set in my mom's basement, and I didn't feel a thing."

"That's terrible," I said, "but I'm glad you made it back. Won't we need the CO_2 later if we have to extinguish a fire?"

"It won't take much to fill the bag," Shun assured me. "Carbon dioxide is very effective at displacing oxygen, so we'll still have plenty left for emergencies."

We got to work. I emptied one of the larger bags while Rodney fetched some duct tape and Shun brought out the canisters we planned to use to kill the insects. Once all the equipment was ready, we suited up in as much protective gear as we could find. I may have gone a bit overboard, layering on my thickest thermal trousers, a waterproof jacket with a padded lining, and, to top it off, a heavy-duty raincoat.

I finished the outfit with two pairs of socks tucked into knee-high rubber boots, double-layered gloves, and an improvised scarf—made from the sleeping bag case—wrapped snugly around my neck. Three layers of mosquito nets draped over my hat, covering my face. Essentially, I was wearing every piece of clothing I had packed, and then some.

Shun laughed when she saw me. "It looks like you're about to embark on a polar expedition!"

"I'm not taking any chances." I squinted through the dull light and the layers of netting to make out Shun's figure. "I'll show you the way to the nest. And Rodney, don't forget the spade."

The nest appeared calmer than before, just as Rodney had predicted—though it was hard to tell if that was the reality or just my poor vision playing tricks on me.

With the bag in hand, Shun and I carefully approached the nest, while Rodney stood ready with the spade to shovel it inside. We crouched down slowly, positioning the bag's opening toward the nest. My pulse quickened with each passing second. I couldn't see or feel them yet, but I knew the bugs were crawling all over me.

"That's it," I said. "Now it's up to you, Rodney. Try to be as gentle as possible so we don't anger them."

The moment he began detaching the nest from the old tree, chaos erupted. The insects swarmed around us, buzzing furiously near our ears. Several clung to the mosquito net, their pincers poised, trying to bite through. I tried blowing them away, but they wouldn't budge. One small gap—around my neck, sleeves, or pant legs—would be enough, and I'd be toast. Just thinking about it made me feel like something was crawling on my skin. I knew it was probably just my mind deceiving me, but that didn't stop me from nearly having a panic attack. Meanwhile, Rodney carefully tipped the nest toward the bag, making sure to scoop up a layer of soil along with it.

"There!" I exclaimed as I felt the weight of the nest drop into the bag. "Quick, seal it!"

In one swift motion, Shun zipped it shut, then flicked on a flashlight, placing it on the ground as she grabbed the CO_2 canister. The muffled buzzing of the insects inside the bag filled the air.

"Open it slightly," Shun instructed. "I'll insert the hose. Rodney, get the duct tape ready."

With a hard swallow, I unzipped the bag about two and a half centimeters. Immediately, two bugs escaped and flew straight toward my face. I had to fight the urge to flail my arms in panic. Shun swiftly inserted the hose, and I zipped the bag tightly around it. Rodney then wrapped several layers of duct tape over the opening.

"Here goes nothing," Shun said as she began filling the bag with gas.

Slowly, the buzzing inside the bag faded, and when it finally went silent, we removed the hose and sealed the bag tightly once more.

"Where should we dispose of it?" I asked as we stood up.

"We should take it back to camp so we can study them," Shun suggested.

Rodney nodded. "Agreed."

"Hold on a minute," I said, raising a hand. "I'm not sure I want those creatures anywhere near me. What if some of them aren't dead yet?"

"Trust me," Shun replied. "They're dead. But if it makes you feel better, we can leave the bag here overnight and pick it up in the morning."

"I'd prefer that," I said.

We walked a few meters away and carefully checked each other for bugs before heading back to camp to undress. Once I finally peeled off my suffocating outfit, I took a deep breath of relief—though the lingering dread of hidden insects continued to haunt me.

Now that the day's work was finally done, we had a moment to take in the view. The black mountain was no longer black. It shimmered with a haunting blue glow, as if reflecting the starry sky above.

"Bioluminescence," Shun said. "Astonishing!"

"You can see it on the animals flying above, too," I added. "Like giant fireflies. And look—at the base—do you see that?"

A faint bluish glow emanated from within the forest surrounding the mountain.

"It's everywhere," Shun whispered.

We slowly lifted our eyes to the sky, and it was unrecognizable. The stars, including our own sun, were positioned differently in the Milky Way in this time period. Some of the stars we were seeing no longer existed in our own time, though we couldn't tell which ones. What fascinated me most, however, were the celestial bodies that looked exactly the same.

It took us a while to piece it together, but we eventually spotted Jupiter, slowly following its usual path around the sun. We speculated that one of the small dots in the sky might have been Mars. The crescent moon, visible near the horizon, was closer to Earth than in our own era, though it was impossible to tell just by looking.

"Aside from a few craters here and there," I said, "those celestial bodies are the same as they will be sixty-six million years from now. Makes you think, huh?"

"Actually," Rodney said, "at this point, Mars still has active volcanoes, and the rings of Saturn might not have formed yet."

"What's that?" Shun interrupted, pointing to something faint rising over the horizon.

The moment she pointed it out, the hair on the back of my neck stood up. Slowly climbing the night sky was a white dot, surrounded by what looked like a green haze.

"Please tell me that isn't what I think it is," I said.

"It's a comet," Shun replied, "but it's impossible to tell if it's... the one."

"If we watch it over the next few nights," Rodney said, "we should be able to figure out if it's heading our way."

"But we can't see its tail," I said, a cold fear creeping up my spine. "Doesn't that mean it's coming straight for us?"

"Not necessarily," Rodney replied. "The visibility of a comet's tail depends on several factors—its composition, the angle of sunlight, and our perspective from Earth. Just because we can't see the tail right now doesn't mean it's heading straight for us. Let's not jump to conclusions. We'll monitor its trajectory and have a clearer idea in the coming days."

"Speaking of the coming days," Shun interjected, "when do you think we should start looking for potential survivors? The longer we wait—"

"I-I'm still recovering," I stammered. "Honestly, I won't be ready for a rescue mission anytime soon—I'm still feeling tingling in my skin from that bite, and I'm lightheaded from the oxygen- rich atmosphere, or maybe it's from the journey here... Either way, I'm pretty sure—"

"I understand," Shun interrupted. "Given everything, it would be reckless to rush into it. Still, it feels wrong to just abandon any potential survivors. If we wait more than a night, that's essentially what we'll be doing… and it doesn't sit right with me."

"That's the thing," I said. "*Potential* survivors. Even if I were back to full strength, the odds of us being torn apart by that swarm are far higher than the chances of some unprepared Swedes surviving more than a few hours here. Our first priority has to be ensuring our own survival—we haven't even set up camp properly yet. After that, we can start thinking about others."

"It wouldn't just be for their sake," Rodney said. "Increasing our numbers would benefit us, too. But I get your point—right now, it would be incredibly dangerous."

"It still feels awful," Shun added. "We have knowledge, we have weapons—"

"We have to act based on what we know," I said, "not on what we feel. And what we know is that they're almost certainly dead, and if we go searching for them now, we'll likely end up the same way. Let's focus on gathering our strength and making sure we have everything we need to survive here first. In other words, let's save ourselves before we even think about saving anyone else. Frankly, the most reasonable approach is to assume they're all dead and simply keep our eyes open while exploring, just in case we're wrong. Either way, we have no moral obligation to risk our lives—no more than they would have an obligation to try and rescue us. Right?"

Shun looked down at her feet. "It still feels wrong," she murmured. "What do you think, Rodney?"

"I'm not sure about Ian's moral reasoning—it doesn't seem to hold any objective truth, as far as I'm concerned—but when it comes to the odds of us dying versus finding survivors, I think he's right."

Shun nodded solemnly. "It's too bad, really, but I guess you're right."

We crawled into the tent for the night. Without a fire, it was cold, even inside our sleeping bags. My mental exhaustion, like a thick brain fog, mixed with the lingering sense of doom from seeing the comet, made it hard to focus my thoughts. Everything felt uncomfortable. I kept thinking I could still smell the cadaver from earlier, though I couldn't tell if it was that or something else. My beard itched so much it nearly drove me mad. All I wanted was a haircut, a clean shave, and a warm bath.

During the night, we took turns guarding the camp—a routine we'd have to continue until we could reinforce the perimeter further. I was the last on duty, straining my ears for the sound of bells or pebbles, fighting off sleep. Because of that, I was the last to wake up the next morning.

When I finally got up, I found Shun in the research tent, storing the now-dead nest for further study. Rodney was walking around with a cloth, collecting morning dew from the leaves and squeezing it into a plastic bottle. I noticed he had already set up a tarp on some sticks to collect rainwater, if the weather allowed.

"We still need to find a more reliable water source," he said when he saw me. "The water we brought won't last long, and there isn't enough vegetation here to gather much dew. I've already talked to Shun about it, and she agrees it should be our next priority—phase two, as I call it."

"Of course," I said, yawning. "I'm ready to get my hands dirty." That wasn't entirely true—I was still pretty shaken up from yesterday's insect bite. "I suggest we start by checking the hillside for springs. The water should be fresh and easy to access."

"Good idea." Rodney squeezed the cloth one last time and walked over to me. "But first, we should eat and drink. We need to make sure we're energized and well-hydrated before heading out."

We ate some of the canned food we had brought, sitting outside the tent—though I stayed in the entrance, still nervous about what might be lurking in the grass.

"I was thinking we should start by looking for groundwater streams running down the hillside," I said, repeating it for Shun to hear as well. "If we can find one—and I think this climate makes that likely—we wouldn't have to worry so much about trekking far to get water."

"That would be ideal," Shun agreed. "I think we should start with a preliminary drone survey of the hill. If there are any lakes or bodies of water near its base, there's a good chance springs could lead down to them. Plus, we can use the drone footage to create a rudimentary map of the area."

Rodney took a mouthful of canned soup, wiped his lips with his sleeve, and said, "Water will attract a lot of animals, so we need to be cautious when approaching it. Eventually, we might want to relocate somewhere we can dig a well, but that comes with its own risks, of course."

"One day," I said, "we could head down the hill and set up camp around the subway car. It would offer protection from most threats—not even a T-Rex could bite through all that metal. Plus, it would give us a chance to study the wildlife more closely, especially that strange infestation."

"We wouldn't stand a chance against that swarm of pale dinosaurs, even inside the subway car," Shun cautioned. "But if it turns out they're not as dangerous as I fear, it could be an option."

We positioned ourselves facing north, according to my compass—the opposite direction from the subway car and the black mountain. Shun thought it was safer to avoid moving too much in the direction of the swarm.

Rodney started the drone while I watched the live footage on the laptop screen. Shun stood guard, holding one of the guns in case anything jumped out of the bushes. The drone flew down the hill, a bit jerky at first, but Rodney soon steadied it, his hands tightening around the controller. I watched with fascination as the lush vegetation below came into view.

As the drone buzzed overhead, startled creatures took flight from the treetops. I couldn't identify them, but they were unlike any birds from our time—these had likely just begun their evolutionary journey, probably still sporting teeth and claws. Rodney lowered the drone beneath the canopy, now watching the screen with me to help navigate. He steered it over the forest floor, where smaller animals—possibly early mammals—scurried away, fleeing the approaching drone.

"Wait!" I said. "Stop... okay, good. Now turn around and look behind you—I thought I saw something moving between those trees."

Rodney followed my instructions. "I see it too," he said, steering the drone toward the trees. Something white was moving behind them, clearly in motion.

As the drone cleared a few bushes, we finally saw what it was: a majestic waterfall, like the ones I had only seen during a trek in the Norwegian wilderness in my youth.

"Bingo," I said, grinning. "Shun, come take a look at this."

She left her post and joined us for a moment. "It's beautiful," she said. "Is it close by?"

"It's fairly close," Rodney replied, "but we can probably access the stream much nearer." He ascended the drone. "I'll try to follow it up the hill."

He guided the drone over the water, which started as a stream nearly the size of a river. It then split into several smaller streams. He tracked the one that seemed closest to us until it, too, broke into a few springs. He stopped when the water became difficult to spot, most likely because it continued beneath the moss. "Keep your eyes on the forest below," Rodney said. "I'm going to lift the drone above it, and it's essential we see where it reappears." He began raising the drone, and we all watched the forest closely. A group of pterodactyls suddenly soared up from a spot about five hundred meters away, and soon after, the drone appeared—a small black smudge against the blue sky.

"There!" Shun exclaimed, even though we'd all spotted it at the same time. "It's close, but getting there is still going to be pretty dangerous. The terrain isn't exactly ideal."

I pulled out my phone—now permanently disconnected from any network—and took a picture of the drone's position so we wouldn't forget where it appeared. Rodney then guided the drone back, just before the battery would have run out.

We spent the rest of the morning reviewing the drone footage and planning our trip to the stream. None of the animals we spotted on the video looked particularly dangerous, though it was hard to make out their details. They wouldn't stand a chance against our guns and would likely be hesitant to approach us anyway. What concerned me most, however, were the unknown creatures that didn't show up on the footage.

We stayed close together, guns in hand, as we descended the hill and made our way toward the stream. It was crucial to stay as quiet as possible, so we spoke only in whispers, if at all. I couldn't take my eyes off the flora around us. It looked familiar at first glance, but upon closer inspection, it was entirely unrecognizable.

An unexpected sound came from the bushes ahead, stopping us in our tracks. My pulse quickened as I tightened my grip on the gun. It wasn't exactly threatening—just a hollow knocking sound. We tried to circle around the source, but as we rounded the bushes, we found ourselves right in front of it.

What we saw was bizarre: a black, irregular mass hanging from tendrils attached to a treetop, covered in dozens of eyes, all surrounded by a putrid stench of decay that hit us like a wave.

The eyes protruded from the dark, amorphous mass like clusters of shimmering orbs, each encased in a translucent membrane that pulsed with a foreboding, inner glow. They varied in size, some as small as marbles, others as large as baseballs, and were scattered haphazardly across the surface of the formless creature. Each eye seemed like a window into an alien world, with irises swirling in hypnotic colors—ranging from vivid violets to deep, impenetrable blacks.

Their pupils weren't round or vertically slit like a cat's; instead, they took the form of intricate geometric shapes—hexagons, spirals, and starbursts—that contracted and dilated in a mesmerizing, unpredictable dance. Each eye darted and swiveled independently, tracking movement with an unsettling precision. The effect was that of a creature in a constant state of heightened awareness, its many gazes seemingly capable of watching in all directions at once.

Also hanging from the tree were two large, insect-like arms ending in massive spikes where hands should have been. Beneath the creature lay a scattering of bones and a partially decomposed carcass, the source of the stench. It was obvious the spikes had killed them, but just as clear was that they weren't prey—the bodies remained untouched.

"What on earth is that?" I whispered.

Shun stepped back, even though we were already far enough to be safe from the spikes. "I don't have a good feeling about this," she murmured.

"It looks like it's made of the same substance we saw on the infected dinosaurs," Rodney said. "But there doesn't seem to be a host—except for all those eyes, and they appear to be part of it rather than attached to something else."

Without warning, every single eye swiveled in unison, fixing their gaze on us.

"It's looking at us," Shun whispered.

"Let's keep moving," I said. "We can come back to study this thing—" The ground trembled. "Do you feel that?"

A menacing screech echoed through the forest, erasing any doubt that something was approaching.

"Cover your ears," Shun commanded, stepping forward with her gun raised. "We can't let it see where we're headed."

She opened fire, riddling the mass of eyes with bullets. The creature swung its spiked arms in defense, but we were far enough away to avoid its reach. Black fluid gushed from the bullet holes, and then, with an internal hiss, the tendrils released the gooey mass. It dropped to the ground and disintegrated, leaving only the eyes behind. I stepped forward and crushed them under my boot, my heart racing as a herd of pale triceratops emerged from between the trees.

"We should probably find somewhere to hide now," Rodney suggested.

"No kidding!" I shouted, breaking into a run. "We need to get the hell out of here."

As we raced down the slope, my heart pounded in my chest, struggling to keep me conscious in the unfamiliar atmosphere I still hadn't acclimated to. I tripped over some roots and fell hard on my arm. I heard it crack, but adrenaline dulled the pain. When I got back to my feet, Rodney was already halfway up a large tree, and Shun stood at its base, ready to climb next.

"Ian!" Shun called, motioning urgently. "Get over here!"

She started climbing, and as soon as she reached the first branch, she extended her hand to me. Wincing from the pain in my arm, I grabbed hold, and she pulled me up just as the triceratops reached us. They thundered past the tree, their heavy steps shaking the ground so violently it felt like the tree might topple.

Once they had stormed by and we could finally catch our breath, the full pain in my arm hit me—it was clearly broken. A few meters away, I heard the soft sound of purling water. By some miracle, our frantic escape had led us right where we needed to be. Even so, we stayed in the tree for a while longer before daring to climb down.

"How's your arm?" Shun asked, noticing the pain on my face as I moved it.

"Broken, I think," I muttered through gritted teeth. I tried to move it again. "Yeah, pretty sure."

"We'll take care of it when we're back at camp," she said. "Do you think you can make it?"

"No worries," I replied, trying to sound confident. "It doesn't hurt that much."

Rodney, still perched on the branch above, chimed in, "Do you think the triceratops charged because that eye-covered organism spotted us? Or was it just bad luck?"

"The swarm attacked right after those eyes locked on us," Shun said. "I don't think that was a coincidence."

"What the hell are we up against here?" I asked. "Do you really think that... thing alerted the herd to our location?"

"We're facing a life form that seems to have evolved a highly effective way to protect itself—possibly even to propagate itself," Shun replied.

"But how?" I pressed. "Can evolution even allow for a creature like that? One capable of controlling not just one, but several hosts at once?"

"And bringing extinct species back to life," Shun added. "It's hard to say how any of this is possible, but one thing's for sure... it's connected to our journey here in some way."

We eventually climbed down—an arduous task for me, even with Shun's help—and approached the stream flowing down the hillside. Rodney crouched and collected some water in a small test tube.

"That's it," he said, holding it up to the light. "It looks clear, no visible organisms, but we'll need to get it back to camp for more thorough testing."

I could barely breathe as we made our way back up the hill. If the pale, slimy swarm returned, I wouldn't stand a chance. With the pain in my arm at its peak, climbing was out of the question. We moved slowly, trying to stay silent, pausing at every sound to look around. Closer to the hilltop, Rodney rushed ahead toward the camp, still avoiding any physical contact, leaving Shun to assist me as we climbed the cliff leading to the summit. My anxiety didn't ease until Shun finally pulled me up. I collapsed onto my back, taking a deep breath of relief.

"Let's go," Shun said. "We need to take care of your arm."

None of us were doctors, but we knew we had to do something about my broken arm. Shun, with her hair tied back in a focused ponytail, held open a medical textbook we'd brought, her eyes scanning the section on fractures. Meanwhile, Rodney hurriedly sifted through our first aid kit, pulling out a roll of gauze and a bottle of disinfectant.

"It says here we need to immobilize it," Shun said, her finger tracing the lines of text. She glanced around and spotted a sturdy, straight branch nearby. "That'll work for a splint," she said, motioning for Rodney to pick it up.

While Rodney stripped the branch of twigs and rough edges, Shun carefully examined my arm. Though she was gentle, her touch still made me wince. "Looks like a closed fracture—no broken skin. That's good; less chance of infection," she remarked.

Rodney returned with the improvised wooden splint in hand. With Shun's guidance, he positioned it along my forearm, from elbow to just past my wrist, carefully avoiding any direct contact with my skin. Together, they tightly wrapped the gauze around my arm and the splint, securing it firmly in place. The goal was to keep my wrist and fingers in as natural a position as possible, minimizing movement to prevent further injury.

Pain flared as they secured the splint, but they were careful, constantly referring back to the textbook and double-checking each step. Once satisfied with the alignment, Rodney used the remaining bandage to wrap around the makeshift brace, adding extra support. They then elevated my arm on a pack to help reduce the swelling.

Despite the difficult situation and our lack of medical expertise, Shun and Rodney's resourcefulness gave me a sense of hope. Once my arm was taken care of, I was reduced to being little more than an observer, possibly for the next month. I could still handle some of the routine tasks around camp, but anything more strenuous was out of the question.

We spent a few hours analyzing the water before finally deciding it was safe to drink—at least after running it through our purifier, though it might even have been fine without it. This was a relief, as it meant we wouldn't die of thirst. However, it also meant we'd have to regularly face the risk of going down there again to collect it.

It was late afternoon, but there was no time for rest. We immediately started on the next task—what Rodney called "phase three"—building the oven. Shun, who had already started digging into the ground to prepare the site, informed me that she and Rodney had settled on building a Dakota Fire Hole while

I was recovering from the insect bite. The goal was to create a fire pit that would be protected from rain, minimize the risk of wildfire, and divert the smoke as much as possible.

I did as much as I could with my right arm and hand, though it was far less than I wanted to contribute. Often, I had to stand by, watching them work, unable to help. Occasionally, I stepped away to look for other tasks I could manage, but there weren't many that needed attention. I felt useless, and despite Shun's reassurances that I didn't need to worry, it still felt like I was being a burden.

They joined me behind the research tent as the sun began to set, casting warm orange rays across the valley below.

"It's beautiful, isn't it?" Shun said.

I couldn't help but feel a twinge of irritation. They had already seen this view, and somehow, that made me feel excluded—as if I'd been left out, though it wasn't anyone's fault but those damn bugs. "It is," I replied, though she didn't meet my gaze. Her eyes were fixed on the horizon, the setting sun casting a soft glow across her face—the only real beauty left in this world. I wished I could've told her that, even as a simple, platonic observation about our unusual circumstances. But I figured it would just make things awkward between us. Besides, I wasn't exactly in the best shape, and it would take more confidence than I could muster to express my feelings. I didn't despair, not even about my broken arm. There was still time. All we had to do was stay alive, and eventually, I'd regain my strength.

Constructing the oven proved to be an arduous task, not just for me but for all three of us. We continued early in the morning, with Shun and Rodney tackling the main hole with admirable energy. Their shovels cut through the earth, creating a hole about a foot deep and equally wide. I did what I could to help, but mostly, I offered words of encouragement, handed them water when needed, and tried to be as useful as possible despite my limited capabilities.

Next, they started on the air tunnel. This hole was smaller and had to be dug about a foot away from the main one. Shun took on most of this task, her small frame making it easier to work in the confined space. It was slow going, and I could see the strain on her face as she pushed herself to dig faster. Meanwhile, Rodney had already begun working on the connecting tunnel. His movements were precise and deliberate despite the physical strain, a clear reflection of his rigorous exercise routine.

By mid-afternoon, they had successfully connected the two holes. Shun, drenched in sweat and dirt, finally straightened up with a satisfied smile on her face. Seeing her, so hardworking and dedicated, gave me a sense of comfort. Despite everything we were facing, we were still capable of accomplishing something—not just surviving, but creating.

They then lined the holes and tunnel with stones, creating a secure structure that would help prevent the walls from collapsing. The stone-lined pit looked sturdy and promising. As they added kindling and firewood to the main hole, I stood aside, watching as they successfully started a fire in our newly built Dakota Fire Hole. The warmth radiating from the flames was comforting, and the fire itself felt like a beacon of hope in our isolated world.

The final touch was placing a small grill over the main hole, ready for the cooking that would inevitably follow. As we sat around the fire, our faces lit by its warm glow, the pain in my arm seemed to ease, replaced by a quiet sense of achievement. I suggested we could hunt small mammals, as hunting dinosaurs was too dangerous. But Shun immediately objected.

"I don't think that's a good idea," she said. "Mammals?"

"What do you mean?" I asked. "They're small and much easier to capture."

"We don't know which species might be our earliest mammal ancestor," she explained. "What if the one we kill carries a mutation that's crucial for humanity's evolution?"

It was hard for me to think clearly. I didn't feel like myself in that regard. Before we arrived here, I considered myself a fairly intelligent person, but now my thoughts seemed to move through maple syrup, especially when faced with complex ideas like time paradoxes. I felt sluggish, slow, and dull. I hadn't yet adjusted to the oxygen levels, at least not as well as Shun and Rodney seemed to have. I pressed my hands to my forehead and tried to focus as hard as I could.

"O-okay," I stammered, "but our trip here already happened. We found the subway car, so whatever we do here—" I paused, trying to gather my thoughts. "We already know it won't stop humanity from evolving."

"Maybe that's because we decided not to eat any mammals," Shun replied. "Let's not tempt fate, okay?"

I closed my eyes, straining to think. "This is making my head hurt. What were we even talking about? Oh, right—food. What do you suggest we eat?"

"To start with... insects," Shun replied. "Insects and other bugs."

"No," I said, instantly more alert. "Just no." The mere thought of what she suggested made me feel sick. "I don't want to go near any more insects here, and I already told you—eating insects is off the table for me. I did it once, hated it, and I'm pretty sure I'll hate it even more now, especially after that run-in with the earwig!" I pressed my hand to my forehead, feeling faint as my arm throbbed with pain. "I'm sorry... I think I need to lie down for a bit."

"Obviously, you're not obligated to adopt an insect-based diet if you don't want to," Shun said, "but it would be a reliable food source given our current situation. But don't worry—I wasn't suggesting we rely solely on bugs. We need a balanced diet, so we'll also forage for fruits, vegetables, and possibly edible roots. And once we're more familiar with the area, we should find a lake and try our luck at fishing."

"There should be one exception to your reluctance to kill mammals," Rodney said. "Since they're our closest relatives here, we could capture a specimen and use it as a kind of canary. We'd give it samples of our food to check for toxicity. If it survives, there's a good chance it's safe for us. If it dies or refuses to eat, we'll know to avoid that type of food."

Shun considered this. "That's a valid point. We should set up a trap using some of our food first thing tomorrow."

"A spring snare would probably be the easiest trap to set up," Rodney said. "It's a pretty simple design. I learned about it from *The Bushcraft Field Guide to Trapping, Gathering, and Cooking in the Wild*. Unfortunately, I didn't have it with me when we got here, but I memorized the important parts, so we should be fine."

"I know how to make one too," I added, "so don't worry if you forget something."

Rodney smiled. "Thanks, Ian."

I finally managed to sleep for a few hours that night, though my dreams were plagued by nightmares of prehistoric insects crawling all over me. When they reached my face, creeping into my mouth, nose, and ears, I jolted awake in a cold sweat. The sun was just beginning to rise and Shun had finished her watch.

"Good morning," she said, her face showing concern. "You were talking in your sleep. It didn't sound pleasant. How are you holding up?"

"I'm not sure," I replied. "My arm feels a bit better, so that's something, but I think I'll lose my mind if I don't get some proper sleep soon."

"Try to get a bit more rest," she suggested. Then she called, "Rodney!" He slowly sat up, stretching his arms.

"It's your turn to stand guard," Shun said. "I'll try to sleep until the sun is at its peak."

After she'd rested, we began preparing for our task. Our kit was simple but essential: a sharp knife, sturdy cordage, and a small piece of dried meat from our limited food supply. Rodney assumed the role of instructor, a position I would have taken myself if not for my broken arm. While he was practically an encyclopedia of knowledge, the wilderness was proving to be a challenging test of his skills–just as I had predicted.

The air was crisp as Rodney led us away from the relative safety of our hilltop camp. His steps were a bit clumsy, and he nearly stumbled several times, but his eyes were sharp as he scanned the environment for any signs of small mammals. He focused on locating a spot near a water source or a patch of dense vegetation, where wildlife might be more active.

Rodney chose a spot by a babbling brook close to our usual water source, nestled within the dense, emerald-green forest. Overhead, the canopy of trees concealed us from view, while below, the forest floor bore the telltale signs of small creatures—tiny, hasty footprints hinting at the hidden life within the undergrowth.

With the location chosen, we set to work constructing the trap. Rodney moved directly to a young sapling, testing its flexibility and strength—it was perfect for a spring snare. Meanwhile, Shun focused on driving a stake into the ground, which would serve as the fulcrum for the trigger bar. They both moved with purpose, turning theory into action.

With my arm still in a splint, my role was mostly supportive. I offered words of encouragement and handed over materials when needed, passing cordage or holding a piece of wood steady as Shun whittled it down. I also kept a vigilant eye on our surroundings, watching for any predators that might be sneaking up on us, ready to shout for Shun to drop everything and grab her rifle if necessary.

We all understood, without needing to say it aloud, not to invade Rodney's space. He still wasn't comfortable with unnecessary touch. His movements were methodical and precise, almost robotic—a quiet rhythm we had come to respect, much like the invisible boundary surrounding him, which we navigated with nods, brief hand gestures, and concise communication.

"This reminds me of my time as a Boy Scout," I said, watching them work. "That's where I learned how to make these kinds of traps." I smiled at the memory. "We picked up all sorts of useful skills, though I've forgotten most of them. Would've come in handy now."

"How'd you forget?" Rodney asked, genuinely surprised.

"Well," I began, "other things started occupying my mind when I hit puberty. You know how it is—" I paused, realizing he might not actually relate to that experience at all.

"And what were those things?" Shun asked teasingly. "What exactly made you give up your promising Boy Scout career?"

I blushed and shook my head. "Well, you know... a lot of things happen at that age, and—"

"I think he's referring to girls," Rodney said matter-of-factly. "Puberty is when sexual preferences start to emerge, which—especially for boys—can completely shift attention away from previous interests. It's likely that Ian, during puberty, became overwhelmed by—"

"Okay, that's enough," I interrupted. "Let's focus on the task at hand."

Shun burst out laughing, covering her mouth to avoid alerting any nearby predators.

Rodney, confused, looked up from where he was working. "Did I say something funny?"

"No," I interjected, still blushing, "not at all. Let's just get back to work, okay?"

With that, we refocused and set about attaching the sapling to the stake with the cordage, creating the spring mechanism. Rodney then carefully whittled a branch into a trigger bar, the crucial piece that would hold the snare's tension and release it when disturbed. The bar was tied to a noose, which we positioned over what we believed to be a likely path for a small mammal.

Once the final touches were in place, we scattered leaves over the cordage, camouflaging the trap. We left the area as stealthily as we had entered, the trap blending seamlessly into the surrounding foliage. We were hopeful that by the next day, we would have our test subject for the gathered food. Still, we were well aware of nature's unpredictability, and the outcome ultimately rested in her capricious hands.

Back at camp I set to work constructing a makeshift cage. The pain in my arm had dulled to a constant throb, a presence my mind had almost grown accustomed to, but it still hampered my efforts, turning what should have been a simple task into a more complicated chore. I gathered thin, flexible branches from the underbrush, carefully selecting each one for its sturdiness and pliability. Awkwardly wielding my knife in my good hand, I began whittling the branches, trimming off smaller offshoots and smoothing the bark. The gentle rustle of the wilderness became a soothing backdrop as I focused on my task. Then came the weaving, the part I knew would be the most challenging. Carefully, I began interlacing the branches, bending and twisting them to form the cage's walls. It was painstaking work, especially with just one hand, but I moved slowly, letting patience guide me. Finally, I crafted a hinged opening, securing it with vines that acted as a natural lock. By the time the sun began to set, a serviceable cage—rough around the edges but sturdy—stood before me.

While I worked on the cage, Shun and Rodney decided to forage for food. We could have survived for about a week on the supplies we'd brought, assuming we rationed carefully, but Shun believed it was important to learn how to live off the land as quickly as possible—better to do so with full stomachs than to wait until we were desperate. Once I finished the cage, I struggled to find something useful to occupy my time, and as the hours passed, a creeping sense of uselessness began to settle in.

I wandered around the campsite, jumping whenever bugs zipped by, each time flashing back to the moment I was bitten. After a while, when I figured Shun and Rodney should have returned, I reached for the walkie-talkie to call them. No immediate reply. Fear began to creep in, and I strained my ears, listening for any sounds of screams or gunshots from the forest below. Half an hour passed—though it felt like an eternity. My heart pounded in my throat, and I even considered climbing down the hill to search for them.

Finally, the radio crackled to life. "Sorry for the radio silence," Shun's voice came through. "We couldn't risk being exposed. I'll explain more when we're back at camp. Over and out."

I sighed with relief and put on my hat, which I hadn't even noticed I'd taken off. When I heard them approaching up the hillside, I rushed over to help, offering my good hand as they climbed the cliffs.

"What happened? Is everything okay?" I asked. "It's getting dark, and I don't think you should be out of camp after—"

"We encountered something... how should I put it?—unsettling," Rodney said, his face showing an unusual expression of concern.

"It was the body of one of the passengers," Shun added, looking equally distraught. "A little boy. He must have survived longer than the others to make it that far. We couldn't determine the cause of death, but..." She hesitated. "He was covered in that black substance, almost like it was growing on him. We removed as much as we could before burying him, but a lot of it had fused to his skin. We had to stay quiet while we were there, which is why we turned off the walkie-talkies and couldn't report back sooner."

"Th-that's horrible," I stammered. "I guess we were wrong about everyone being killed by the swarm. It must have taken a miracle for him to escape. Do you think there could be other survivors?"

"Impossible to say," Rodney replied. "Maybe."

"We'll need to stay alert," Shun added, "but we can't risk a rescue mission based on the slim chance that someone else might still be alive—not right now, at least."

Relieved that she didn't suggest searching for other possible survivors, I said, "Agreed. And I think you did the right thing burying the boy, even if it was risky." Glancing down at their bags, I added, "Anyway, I'm dying to know if you found anything to eat."

"We did," Shun replied with a smile, holding up a plastic container. Inside were what looked like oversized berries—though they didn't quite resemble anything I had seen before.

"And check these out!" Rodney said, holding up something that looked like pink, translucent raisins. "I saw a mouse-like animal eating them, so we tasted a few. They're pretty bitter. Try one!" He offered me the container with a grin.

"Interesting," I said, popping one into my mouth. As I chewed, I added, "You weren't kidding—they're really bitter." I had to resist the urge to rinse my mouth with our precious water. "Did you find anything else?"

"Only this," Shun said, handing me their bag. "You're not going to like it."

She wasn't wrong. Inside was a creature about thirty centimeters long, with an elongated, segmented body and rows of slender, translucent legs lining its sides. Thankfully, it was dead.

"Where did you find it?" I asked, grimacing.

"We tipped over a boulder and found several of them underneath," Rodney replied, sounding more impressed than I thought was appropriate. "They were hiding there—probably nocturnal."

"I've never seen anything like it," I said, turning the creature over with a stick. "Those segmented legs... the chitinous body... It's like a cross between a shrimp and a centipede. Any thoughts, Shun?"

Shun, ever the arthropod enthusiast, her eyes gleaming with fascination, replied, "It looks like some sort of myriapod, but the size and body structure don't match anything I know of from this time period."

Rodney grinned. "Maybe we just discovered a new species."

"Perhaps," Shun replied, still studying the creature. "But without knowing more, we can't be sure if it's safe to eat."

"Hopefully," Rodney said, "we'll catch something by tomorrow to test if it's safe."

I gave him a flat look. "I think I'll pass either way. I'd rather stick to the fruits and berries until we find something that doesn't look like it escaped from a mad scientist's lab."

"Again, it's your choice," Shun said, pulling back from the creature and tucking it into her bag. "But we can't afford to be too picky out here. Either way, we need to document this discovery and gather more specimens if possible. It could be a groundbreaking find—edible or not."

To our delight, we found a small mammal in our trap the next day. It looked like a shrew or vole, small and unassuming. We placed it in my makeshift cage and headed back to camp. Its fur was a soft blend of dusty brown and cream, and its beady eyes sparkled with intelligence. As I gently picked it up, it wriggled in my hands, its tiny claws scratching against my skin. But soon its fear subsided, and it began sniffing around, perhaps sensing that we meant no harm. The creature had an unusually long snout, more so than any rodent I'd ever encountered, which twitched constantly as it picked up scents unknown to us.

Back at camp, Shun watched with unabashed fascination as the little mammal darted around the cage, its nose sniffing the air and tiny paws scratching at the bottom. For a fleeting moment, its charming antics made me forget my desperate circumstances.

"What are we going to call it?" Shun asked, leaning in to observe our new resident.

Rodney, who had been quiet until then, offered, "How about Dash 8?"

Shun and I both looked at him, surprised.

"What's that?" I asked.

"It's a series of diesel-electric freight locomotives," he explained.

I smiled. "Come on, Rodney, we can't name it after a train."

"Let's just stick with Dash, shall we?" Shun said, placing a hand on my shoulder with a grin.

Dash seemed to settle into its new home, unfazed by our attention. Its confidence was oddly reassuring, almost uplifting. As it turned out, while we sat around the fire later, all the food Shun and Rodney had gathered was edible; at least, if we could trust our little early warning system. Unfortunately, it wasn't very appetizing. The fruits tasted like raw leaves, and the meat from the centipede-like creature—which I forced myself to eat for the sake of morale—was reminiscent of rancid eel. I nearly threw up trying to swallow.

"Now we can finally focus on our research," Shun said as we sat around the fire. "I'd really like to collect some of that black slime to figure out what it is."

"That shouldn't be hard," Rodney replied. "It seems to be everywhere in this environment."

"True," I agreed. "But messing with it could be extremely risky. What if it makes us sick—or worse, turns us into one of those pale abominations?" I shuddered at the thought. "There's plenty to study here. Maybe we should take it slow with the Lovecraftian slime, don't you think?"

"Safety will be our top priority," Shun said, "but I don't think we can afford to wait. I have a feeling that it wants to study us just as much as we want to study it, and it already has samples of our species. We need to level the playing field—and fast. Remember, it knows we're alive."

"That's assuming it has human-like intelligence," I said. "Which seems unlikely to me. I mean... thinking slime? It's more likely that it operates purely on instinct. It probably just consumed the remains of the others."

"In either case," Rodney said, "it's clearly the most interesting life form we've discovered here—more fascinating than the dinosaurs, even. If my hunch is right, these types of organisms typically use spores to infest their hosts, which means just by breathing the air, we could be at risk. Figuring out its method of infection could be crucial for reducing that risk or at least understanding it better."

"Spores?" My eyes widened. "That's it! I'm wearing the N95 from now on. Seriously, I don't want to turn into one of those things."

"I'm not sure that's how it works," Shun said, taking another bite of the gray, slippery meat. "Think about it—we've seen it control species that should be extinct. If it relied on spores, it would've had to find those hosts in the environment. And what about that mass with all the eyes? That didn't seem like an infected organism; it felt like something entirely unique. Right?"

"Wait a minute," I said, trying to process. "What exactly are you saying?"

"I don't have a clear explanation," Shun replied, "but it's obvious that this organism isn't just spreading spores into the lungs of local fauna. Still, I agree with Rodney—whatever it is, we need to study how it operates."

I sighed. "Let's at least wait until my arm has healed. We shouldn't take any risks while we're one person short. In the meantime, there's still plenty to do around camp. We could build an outhouse, create storage for the weapons and other supplies—and maybe even a shower! I could really use a proper wash. After everything we've been through, we're beyond filthy."

"Alright," Shun said, nodding. "That's fair. Another thing we should consider building is a lookout further down the hill, maybe near that waterfall—or if there's a lake nearby, we could set it up there. Just a simple wooden platform in one of the trees. From that vantage point, we could study the surroundings and even use our fishing gear safely." A smile appeared on her lips. "I really believe we can carve out a life here. Sure, it'll be harsh and unpredictable, but also filled with discoveries that would've stayed buried in the sands of time if we hadn't been thrown into this prehistoric era. Just a few weeks ago, we were studying fossils and debating theories in the safety of our universities—and you, Rodney, were probably sitting at home reading about trains. Now, we're living a theory, a wild, surreal dream that's become our reality."

In the quiet of the night, with the fire crackling and alien stars overhead, I reflected on how much life had changed. My skin still tingled and burned occasionally from the insect bite, keeping me from sleep. My broken arm ached with every movement, and the oxygen-rich atmosphere left my mind in a constant haze. Unlike Shun, I wasn't quite ready to consider us lucky—though I was trying.

"Sure," I began hesitantly, "there's something about this primitive life. I guess we're more in tune with nature, and everything feels more... raw. Living here makes you realize how easy things were in our time and how much we took for granted. It's a bit of a wake-up call about what life really is—just trying to survive, I suppose. It makes you appreciate life more."

My attempt to convince myself, to rationalize our predicament, fell flat. But Shun's smile as she looked at me made it worth it. Maybe, in time, those words would become true.

We stayed close to camp during most of my recovery, with the only exceptions being when Rodney and Shun ventured out to gather water from the spring or forage for food. They never went far and only stayed outside the camp as long as absolutely necessary. Stuck at camp, I kept myself occupied by preparing the food they brought back and starting an ambitious project:

building an outhouse—a simple but much-needed addition to our site. Once that was finished, which took a day and a half, I moved on to laying the groundwork for a makeshift shower system, a few paces downhill from the main camp.

The shower setup was rudimentary at best, but it would do the job. First, I found a sturdy tree branch strong enough to hold a container full of water. When I couldn't find the perfect branch, I improvised by fashioning a stand from sturdy poles, interlaced and bound tightly with strips of bark and vines.

Next, I modified one of our water containers, attaching a small, salvaged piece of hose to serve as a makeshift showerhead. With the stand in place and the modified container ready, I hoisted the empty vessel onto the stand—a task that was easier said than done with my arm still in a splint.

With the higher parts of the shower setup complete, I moved on to ensuring some privacy. Using a spare tarp and a few more poles, I constructed an open-ended enclosure around the shower area. The open side allowed easy access and provided a way for the water to drain away, while the tarp shielded the user from the prying eyes of any curious wildlife.

Throughout the process, one thing remained clear: we'd have to get used to cold showers unless we found a way to heat the water. But that was a problem for another day. For now, our simple yet functional shower system was complete. In the midst of this prehistoric wilderness, having even this small modern comfort felt like a significant victory.

It bothered me a bit to be stuck at camp for so long, but from a research perspective, it wasn't a huge issue. The view over the valley gave us plenty of opportunities to study the wildlife from a safe distance. We spotted a variety of species we thought we recognized—Sonorasaurus, Hadrosaurus, Colepiocephale, and healthy Triceratops, among others—but to our delight, most of the species were unfamiliar to us, turning each sighting into a fascinating discovery. This wasn't surprising, of course, given that only about one percent of species from this time are represented in the fossil record. In fact, what surprised us was that we could identify any dinosaurs at all.

We only saw what we called the swarm of infected dinosaurs a few times. They appeared intermittently, hunting, then returning with their prey to the nest.

Despite these sightings, Shun's idea of building a lookout was still up for discussion. During one of their trips, she and Rodney had ventured all the way down to the waterfall and discovered a lake, where she now wanted to construct the lookout.

I urged them to wait until I was better so I could help, but Shun insisted that waiting would be too risky. We were running low on the food we'd brought, and what they'd managed to forage wasn't enough. To have any hope of maintaining a stable diet, we needed to try our luck at fishing. I objected, but the gnawing hunger in my stomach made it clear she was right.

As I watched them set off on their arduous task, their figures disappearing into the verdant maze of undergrowth that led down to the lake, a wave of helplessness and frustration washed over me. This project would keep them away from camp for longer than ever before. Although we communicated via walkie-talkie whenever possible, each hour without their physical presence felt like a lifetime.

Although I couldn't see them from camp, their daily reports painted a vivid picture. With the precision of a watchmaker, they selected a tall, sturdy tree on the lake's edge, just a stone's throw from the waterfall. Its position offered a sweeping view of the water and surrounding terrain—perfect for an observation platform. Rodney, armed with his book knowledge, and Shun with her practical skills, set to work by hauling up lengths of spare rope, using them to create a series of rudimentary footholds around the tree.

Over the next several days, they secured a stable platform high in the branches. Built from a sturdy wooden frame and overlaid with a woven mesh of branches and leaves, the solid base was just big enough for three people to recline and observe the area below.

Meanwhile, back at camp, the weight of solitude grew heavier with each passing day. Though I tried to distract myself, focusing on tasks I could manage one-handed, the specter of isolation haunted my every moment.

The lush prehistoric wilderness around me, once filled with wonder, began to feel like an immense, oppressive cage. Every chirp of an unseen insect or rustle from an unknown creature only reminded me of how utterly alone I was in this vast, ancient world.

Shun and Rodney's expeditions started in the earliest hours of dawn, when the sky was still painted with twilight, and lasted until dusk settled in. During those long, seemingly endless hours, I found myself grappling with a torrent of thoughts: *Would they encounter a creature they couldn't escape from? A terrain they couldn't navigate?* Every unexpected crackle from the walkie-talkie made my heart jump, half-expecting it to carry a cry for help or signal some disaster.

But beyond the immediate fears, deeper, more introspective worries crept in. *Was my confinement to the camp causing me to miss the moments that would define this adventure? Would future campfire stories recount adventures and discoveries I had no part in?* The sense of missing out, of being on the fringes of our shared experience, was perhaps harder to bear than the physical challenges themselves.

However, with each setting sun, a wave of relief would wash

over me. As the fiery orange hues of twilight gave way to the darkening canopy above, their voices would crackle through the walkie-talkie, puncturing my fears with a breath of tangible relief.

It took four days for them to finish most of the lookout. When they returned on the fourth day, their faces flushed with effort and their eyes gleaming with accomplishment, I knew it had been worth it. As always, they came back with detailed notes and observations of new species, but this time they carried a renewed sense of purpose as well. Their achievement had clearly improved our situation, and while I was glad for that, I couldn't help but wish I'd been part of it instead of stuck at the main camp, nursing my injury from the sidelines.

Sitting around the fire that evening—still eating tiny berries, the gray goo from the shrimp-like centipedes, and the last of our canned food since they hadn't yet attempted fishing in the lake—I felt a deep sense of relief that the lookout was finally complete. Now, I hoped, things would take a turn for the better. With the extra food we expected from the lake, I thought I might even regain the remaining bits of my physical and mental strength.

"Given the swarm's seemingly intelligent coordination," Shun said, more to Rodney than to me, "and the unchecked spread of the slime, it's a mystery why it hasn't taken over the entire planet."

My mental fatigue left me pretty useless when it came to solving mysteries, but I could still listen and grasp what they were discussing.

"The most reasonable explanation," Rodney said, "is that it needs some parts of the environment to remain untouched—most likely to preserve its food supply."

"That would require an incredible ability to think ahead," I said. "The idea of a slime mold, fungus, or whatever it is being capable of that, even in this bizarre situation, is hard to believe."

"I don't know," Shun mused. "Maybe."

Later, before bed, I studied the sky as usual and noticed the comet had disappeared completely. An immense sense of relief washed over me, as if a death sentence hanging over my head had been lifted. Still, even with that weight gone, my sleep didn't improve. Once again, I woke up in the middle of the night after dreaming of being consumed by flames in an apocalyptic inferno, startling Shun and drawing Rodney's attention from outside, where he was standing guard.

"I'm sorry," I said. "It was just another nightmare." They took it well enough, but I noticed a hint of irritation on Shun's face. This wasn't the first time I had accidentally woken her, and though she didn't say anything, I could tell it was starting to get on her nerves.

"You know what," I offered, "I think I should try sleeping in the research tent."

"No, it's okay," Shun said. "You don't need to—"

"I think it would be for the best," I insisted, secretly hoping she'd argue against it some more. "I don't want to ruin your sleep any more than I already have."

"Well," she said sleepily, "if you go, just be careful with the boxes near the entrance—those samples are fragile."

A part of me felt disappointed, but I grabbed my bedroll and sleeping bag and did my best to push it aside. Lying under the orange ceiling of the research tent, I found myself thinking about life back home. For a brief moment, I wondered what my friends were up to and which team was winning the Stanley Cup Finals, as if I'd simply traveled to a far-off land. But then it hit me—my friends weren't doing anything, and no one was playing for the Stanley Cup. That wouldn't happen for another sixty-six million years. In that moment, lying in the research tent by myself, I felt more alone than I ever had before.

A week later, my arm had improved considerably. It was finally time to take off the splint. Though I still needed to be cautious—no heavy lifting or climbing trees—I could participate in our daily routines again, like gathering water and foraging. This small victory boosted my spirits, especially since it meant I could help with the final stages of the lookout project.

The location for the lookout was breathtaking, a serene tableau in the heart of this prehistoric world. A shaft of sunlight pierced the canopy, casting a radiant halo over the waterfall and creating a mesmerizing rainbow in the shimmering mist. The lake, a peaceful expanse of clear water, lay cradled by a fringe of tall, slender trees.

We spent the day putting the final touches on the lookout. Our main focus was reinforcing the platform by weaving additional branches into the floor, giving it greater stability. We also added a protective barrier around the edges, making it safer to move around and sleep. A pulley system was installed to hoist supplies, sparing us the effort of manual hauling.

As the sun dipped below the horizon, painting the sky in hues of orange and pink, we finished our work. I couldn't help but feel a sense of accomplishment as I looked over the completed lookout. Although I had joined the construction late, contributing to the project, even in a small way, felt deeply rewarding.

We barely had time to savor our hard work before something else caught our attention. A sound—unmistakably a dog's bark—echoed up from deeper in the forest. We all tensed. A cold shiver ran down my spine as I struggled to comprehend how it was possible. It took me a few extra seconds to realize, and just as I was about to say it, Shun spoke:

"It must be the dog from the subway... Could it really have survived all this time?"

"It's not impossible," Rodney said, "but I'd say it's unlikely. It's probably infected."

"Well, it depends, doesn't it?" I said. "It's not entirely impossible—especially considering you found the dead boy earlier—that a group from the subway car survived and took care of the dog." A flicker of hope ignited in me at the thought of reuniting with other people, momentarily overshadowing my earlier caution about attempting a rescue. "Let's investigate. Finding others could radically change our situation—for the better, I'd argue. This is a chance we can't miss."

"I agree," Shun said. "As far as I remember, it wasn't a large dog—just a small poodle. If it's infected, it shouldn't pose much of a threat to us."

With that, we grabbed our weapons, filled a few bottles with water, and set off in the direction of the dog's bark—somewhere west of the lake.

"They might get angry with us if they find out we had an idea of what might happen and didn't warn anyone," Rodney said.

"We didn't know for sure," I replied. "We only *suspected* something could happen, and we had no way of knowing when. What were we supposed to do, ask Stockholm public transport to scrap the car?"

"Rodney does have a point," Shun said, keeping a cautious eye on the dense forest around us. "Rationally, we're not to blame for what happened to the passengers, but people rarely think rationally—especially not after a traumatic experience. They're quick to find scapegoats. It won't matter whether we're responsible if we're perceived as such. I suggest we keep quiet about why we were on that subway car, if we find any survivors."

The dog's barking grew louder and clearer as we pressed on. I clenched my teeth, struggling to maintain my composure while we navigated through the thick, tangled underbrush that made the terrain difficult to traverse.

When we reached the spot where we'd heard the dog barking, we stopped abruptly. It was dark—the sun couldn't penetrate the dense tree canopies above. The air buzzed with insects, some of them clearly bloodsuckers, given how persistently they swarmed around our faces. I kept waving my hand to chase them away while gripping my weapon tightly. Shun nodded toward us, signaling that we should move forward into a small clearing filled with alarmingly large spider webs.

Occasionally, something small would fall from the trees, hitting the ground with soft thuds, while faint rustling echoed from the bushes around us. Each sound made us pause, holding our breath for a few tense seconds before moving on. The air smelled musty, like damp leaves and hidden decay. A small flying lizard darted from a branch above, but aside from that brief flash of movement, the forest felt eerily deserted. The dense foliage, interwoven with massive trees, allowed only thin shafts of light to pierce through. Then, the dog barked again—close, but hard to pinpoint. One moment, it sounded like it was just a few meters ahead, then behind us, and finally—impossibly—it seemed to come from above, somewhere in the tree canopies.

"This doesn't feel right," I whispered. "I take back what I said about potential survivors—something else is going on here... and I don't want to know what it is."

"Don't talk so much," Shun whispered back, a hint of irritation in her tone. "Do you see that?" She pointed her weapon toward something black moving down a tree trunk ahead. In the dim light, it was impossible to make out exactly what it was, but the shadowy silhouette was clearly too large to be a small poodle.

The shadowy figure darted quickly to the left before vanishing into the bushes. Almost immediately, the dog's barking came from the same direction as the unknown creature.

"I think Ian's right," Rodney began. "It might be time to head back—"

Before he could finish, something large fell from the treetops, crashing to the ground with a heavy thump. We recoiled in shock, stumbling a few meters backward. Leaves, dust, and debris flew into the air, making it even harder to see in the already dim light. In front of us, the dog barked feverishly as something began to rise from the chaos—eight massive spider legs, sharp as spears, protruding from the back of the small poodle. It was suspended upside down, a solid five meters above the ground, frantically chewing and barking like a rabid beast.

Before we could react, the creature lunged forward. I opened fire as I bolted in the opposite direction, but my panic made it impossible to aim properly. Shun fired too, but her bullets merely ricocheted off the creature's long legs as if they were made of solid bone. There was no time to figure out how to take it down. Shun and Rodney sprinted ahead, moving faster than I could in my adrenaline-fueled state, while I heard the creature's legs tapping ominously behind me.

"Hurry up, Ian!" Shun screamed, attempting to shoot the monster again—this time aiming for its body, the dog. But her shot missed, nearly impossible to land in the chaos.

I tripped over a rock and tumbled forward, landing in a stagnant pool of water that softened my fall, sparing me from further injury. As I turned around, the creature loomed above me, one of its sharp legs raised, ready to strike. Acting on impulse, I aimed at the dog's body suspended above and emptied the entire magazine. The dog let out a pained howl before falling silent—a wave of guilt washed over me. Then, as its warm blood splattered across my face, the monstrous creature collapsed, its legs twitching uncontrollably.

I immediately knelt in the water, groaning from the pain and shock still pulsing through my body, and frantically washed the blood from my face with the foul-smelling water. "What the hell was that?" I exclaimed, the question more to myself than anyone else. "Oh god, oh god, oh god! What was that?" This time, I looked directly at Shun and Rodney, who were now standing around me. "I almost died," I gasped, noticing how fast I was breathing. "It was about to impale me. What *was* that thing?"

"You killed it," Shun said, crouching over the grotesque creature. "Not bad. I don't see any slime on the dog or the spider legs, but it's hard to say for sure without an autopsy. Still, it's possible this is an entirely different, unknown life form—some kind of parasite, maybe." She stood up, walked over to me, and helped me to my feet. "Are you alright?" she asked.

"No, I'm not alright!" I said, frantically checking myself for injuries. "None of this is alright!"

"I mean, under the circumstances—"

"I'm uninjured, yes," I admitted, "but that was disgusting!"

"Let's head back to the lookout," Rodney suggested. "This place could be crawling with more of those creatures, and the others are probably attached to animals far less pleasant than poodles."

The next day, we set out on a new task—crafting fishing rods. While we had brought fishing line, hooks, and various baits from our time, we still needed to find suitable rods. I hoped fishing, aside from providing us a sustainable food source, would give me another task to occupy my mind in this unforgiving environment.

We started by searching the campsite for suitable branches—ones long enough to allow proper casting distance but sturdy enough to handle the weight of a catch. It took some time, but eventually, we found branches with the right balance of resilience and length.

Returning to camp, we carefully set about refining these natural tools. Using our knives, we shaved off the bark and trimmed away any smaller branches, leaving behind sturdy, bare shafts. With precise strokes, we tapered one end to form a handle, while keeping the other end slightly thicker to hold the line. To ensure a comfortable grip and avoid splinters, we meticulously smoothed the handles, sanding them down with rough stones until they were as polished as any store-bought rod.

The next step was attaching the fishing line. At the thicker end of each rod, we carved a small notch to anchor the line, ensuring it wouldn't slip off. We threaded the fishing line through these notches, tying each one securely. Once that was done, we attached hooks to the ends of the lines, ready for baiting.

We descended to the lake, clutching our makeshift fishing gear. The tranquil setting stirred memories of my youth, when my late father would take me fishing in the forest. Our catch was often meager—mostly perch or catfish—but the thrill of the chase never faded. A trace of that old excitement flickered within me now, though it was overshadowed by the danger of this primordial world. Every step away from the safety of camp sent my heart racing. I longed to hurry and reach the secure confines of the lookout, but caution forced us to move slowly, avoiding any unwanted attention. We crept downhill, fingers hovering over the triggers of our firearms, ready to react at a moment's notice.

Once we reached the lookout, a small sense of calm returned within me. We had arrived at our destination, and it was time to shift from cautious travelers to patient fishermen. From the safety and height of the platform, we carefully arranged our fishing gear. We added small, hollow gourds to the lines as makeshift bobbers. These floaters would drift naturally with the water's flow, imitating the movement of live prey, and their sudden plunge beneath the surface would signal a potential catch. With the lines ready, we moved on to baiting the hooks, choosing a variety of options like earthworms and grubs. We carefully threaded the wriggling creatures onto the hooks, making sure they were secure but still lively enough to attract a fish's attention.

It was time to cast our lines. Using the rods' flexibility, we swung our arms back and then quickly forward, releasing the lines and sending them sailing into the sparkling lake waters. Each baited hook landed with a satisfying splash, creating gentle ripples across the surface. The gourd bobbers floated, tugging lightly on the lines as they drifted with the current.

We settled back, propping our freshly crafted rods against the barrier, the lines disappearing into the tranquil waters below. Our eyes stayed fixed on the bobbers, every slight movement sending a jolt of anticipation through us. But fishing requires patience, and we knew we might be there for a while.

As we sat quietly, watching our bobbers and listening to the sounds of nature, the lookout felt more like a haven than ever before. The contrast to our treacherous journey downhill was stark—the intense vigilance had given way to calm anticipation. Here, in the heart of this prehistoric world, we weren't just surviving; we were living. From this high vantage point, we could safely engage in a pastime as old as humanity itself, momentarily free from the ever-present dangers lurking just beyond our sight. For a brief time, it almost made me forget my inner struggles, though they still lingered, buried deep beneath the surface.

Without warning, one of the rods bent sharply—the floater had gone under. Quickly, I grabbed the rod. Whatever we'd hooked was strong, and the pull made my injured arm ache as I struggled to hold on. At the same moment, Shun grabbed the second rod—she had caught something too. The once-calm water rippled around my floater, and it was clear we'd hooked something big, the size of a tuna.

"Rodney!" I called. "Please help!" He hesitated, unsure how to grab the rod without touching me. "Now, Rodney!" I urged.

Rodney finally stepped in, gripping the rod alongside me. "It's heavy!" he grunted, careful to avoid touching my hand as he tightened his grip. We pulled in sync, our muscles straining against the powerful force beneath the water.

Out of the corner of my eye, I saw Shun struggling with her own catch. Her lean muscles were taut with effort, her eyes narrowed in determination. Suddenly, the force on the other end of her line surged. She let out a cry of surprise as her fingers slipped from the rod's handle. It flew into the water with a plunge, disappearing beneath the surface.

"No!" she shouted, lunging after the vanishing rod, but it was too late.

"Don't worry," I started, "we'll make—"

My words were cut off as the line on my rod went taut, snapping me back into my own struggle. The fish surged again, pulling harder. Rodney and I redoubled our efforts, digging our heels into the ground. With the fight reaching its peak, the rod bent dangerously, groaning as if it might snap, but we held firm. Our breaths were ragged, our muscles burning in protest, yet our resolve remained unyielding.

Finally, after what felt like hours, a flash of scales broke the surface, glinting in the afternoon sun. The fish was massive—a beast of a catch. With one last surge of effort, we pulled again.

The fish burst from the water, thrashing wildly as we heaved it onto the wooden platform with a solid thump. Rodney and I staggered backward, exhausted but triumphant.

Shun ran over. "Incredible," she breathed, crouching next to the enormous fish. Its gills flapped weakly, sending droplets of water flicking off its shiny scales. She placed a reverent hand on it, as if paying respect to the life we had just taken.

That night, as we feasted on our catch—after first giving Dash a taste to ensure it was safe—I felt a sense of genuine peace for the first time since our arrival. Though I was still sleep-deprived, plagued by the persistent neuropathic pain in my skin and the dull ache in my arm, and my mind still felt clouded, the emotional turmoil in my chest had finally eased somewhat.

With fishing added to our routine, starvation was no longer a looming threat. This shift allowed us to redirect our focus from mere survival to exploration and research. Of course, given the constant danger, our explorations remained limited, sticking to safer zones like the hillsides and the lake, where quick retreats were possible if needed. Yet, even in these relatively safe areas, we made rich discoveries. We spent hours observing the environment, followed by even more time meticulously documenting and cataloging our findings.

Shun and Rodney approached these tasks with the enthusiasm of true naturalists. For them, all the challenges were justified by the opportunity for discovery. They had fully embraced their new lives, adapting to the circumstances in ways I still struggled to. My constant unease never seemed to truly fade—every moment of hope was followed by twice as many setbacks that dragged me down. Still, I pushed myself to contribute as much as I could, doing my best to bury my inner turmoil and keep our collective spirits from sinking.

During one of our cautious ventures into the forest surrounding the lake, we had an encounter that finally allowed us to collect a sample of the black slime Shun had been eager to examine. It had been some time since we had last come across the substance, likely because we had been intentionally avoiding areas we knew it had spread to.

For reasons we couldn't understand, an army of ants, their white bodies coated in black slime, marched defiantly through the forest. We kept a safe distance, but quick-thinking as ever, Shun managed to trap a few under a plastic container before they vanished into the wilderness. Wearing protective gloves, she carefully sealed the container, and we transported our captured specimens back to camp.

Our investigation of the ants began in earnest. Though biology wasn't our strongest suit, the reference materials we had brought along provided some guidance. Using these resources, we meticulously dissected our observations. Shun was the first to notice how the ants moved in unison, almost as if the black substance were puppeteering their tiny bodies. We couldn't be entirely sure if this was a natural aspect of the ants' behavior or the direct influence of the substance, but it was intriguing nonetheless.

As we delved deeper into our analysis, we made a fascinating—yet unnerving—discovery. Under the microscope, we observed that the substance wasn't merely a coating; it had penetrated the ants, spreading through their bodies in a network-like pattern. We compared this to various illustrations and descriptions of fungal infections from our books, but the patterns didn't match. This wasn't the typical fungal takeover, where fungi colonize a host with a web of filaments. It was something else entirely.

Rodney, who had been quietly flipping through a field guide

on microorganisms, finally spoke up. "Guys, I think this might be a slime mold."

We stared at him in surprise, but he simply pointed to an illustration of a slime mold in the book. Upon closer inspection, the images depicted networks strikingly similar to what we were observing in the ants. The diagrams showed a single-celled organism capable of aggregating and functioning as a multicellular entity when food was plentiful. We couldn't be certain—advanced lab equipment would be needed for that—but our findings aligned with the unusual behavior of slime molds, opening up a whole new set of questions.

"It's just as you guessed from the start, Rodney," Shun said, looking at him with a sense of admiration—a look she had never given me. "You mentioned a specific species earlier..." She paused, trying to recall. "Which one was it—"

"I think you're referring to my favorite slime mold," Rodney said with a slight grin. "It's called Physarum polycephalum. Slime molds are fascinating organisms—despite being unicellular, they show surprising intelligence and adaptability. They can even learn and retain memory, solving complex problems. But none, as far as we know, has ever shown the ability to control other organisms."

Shun nodded. "That aspect certainly adds an unsettling layer to our mystery."

To better understand how the slime interacted with living creatures, we decided to recreate the conditions of infection in a controlled environment. From our collection traps, we selected several specimens—ground beetles, ants, and even an archaic roach species unique to this time period. We placed each in separate clear containers, along with a bit of the black slime, and watched with bated breath as the minute drama unfolded before us.

The reactions, however, were not what we had anticipated.

Though the insects were initially alarmed, they soon settled down, appearing to either ignore or avoid the slime altogether. In turn, the slime showed no obvious interest in them. We watched, bewildered, as hours turned into days with no noticeable changes in the behavior of either the insects or the slime.

"The black substance clearly isn't parasitic," I said, "at least not in the way a fungus would be. It hasn't made any attempt to infect the healthy insects."

"Yet," Shun added, "the ants we found were undeniably consumed by the substance. Could it be that only certain species are vulnerable? Or perhaps the slime needs to reach a certain level of... consciousness before it becomes infectious?"

"Consciousness," I repeated, shaking my head. "I still think you're giving it way too much credit. Without a doubt, it's a sophisticated organism capable of unbelievable things—but that doesn't mean it's acting on anything more than instinct."

"It might be more like a pathogen," Rodney suggested, "waiting to be ingested or come into contact with a vulnerable part of the body before it can infect."

Shun, still clearly considering the possibility of some kind of consciousness, replied, "That's definitely possible, but shouldn't it have found weak spots on the ants in our experiment by now? I'm not sure we can rule out the idea that it might choose which organisms to infect. All I'm saying is we need to keep an open mind."

Despite our best efforts, we were left with more questions than answers. We were trying to comprehend the behavior of a completely alien entity, using the limited ecological and biological knowledge we had. The black slime remained a mystery, defying any known principles of biology we could apply. Its existence, behavior, and apparent selective infection—all of it made no sense. Yet, despite our apprehension, we couldn't help but feel a deep sense of fascination.

A bit later, Shun—no doubt in an effort to maintain the scientific integrity of our mission—suggested a binomial nomenclature for the organism: Cognimyxa dominator.

"What does it mean?" I asked.

"Well..." She glanced at her notes, a smile forming on her lips. "Breaking it down, Cognimyxa combines the Latin cognitio, meaning knowledge, to hint at the slime mold's intelligence, with -myxa, the suffix for slime molds. So, it basically refers to an intelligent slime mold. As for dominator, it comes from the Latin dominatus, meaning 'having been dominated' or 'having ruled.' In this context, it represents the organism's ability to dominate or control other beings. So, Cognimyxa dominator essentially suggests a highly intelligent slime mold capable of exerting control over other organisms."

"It certainly has an... ominous ring to it," I said. "I'm still a bit skeptical about the idea of thinking slime..." I left the sentence unfinished, not wanting to sound overly critical. After all, it was just a name—one that no one but us would ever know—so there was no reason to argue and risk creating a bad atmosphere. "... But yeah, it's a fitting name. Let's stick with it."

She nodded with a satisfied smile and headed back into the research tent. I stood there, returning her smile as I watched her walk away. Then, I turned to face the black mountain on the other side of the valley. "Cognimyxa dominator," I whispered, my smile fading.

As the rhythm of our lives settled into a routine, our days began to blur into a continuous loop. Breakfast at dawn, cooked over the Dakota Fire Hole, became the launchpad for each day. After the meal, one of us would do a quick sweep of the perimeter—a precautionary check for any signs of the black slime or other potential threats. With the camp secure, we began our daily ritual of foraging and fishing. Armed with baskets and fishing gear, we ventured into the forest and down to the lookout. Our tasks were carried out in near silence, each of us knowing our roles and performing them without the need for spoken instructions. The fruits of our labor—wild edibles and fresh catches—were brought back to camp at the end of each outing.

Afternoons were dedicated to maintenance and research. We inspected and repaired our equipment—everything from fishing rods to water purifiers—ensuring it was all in working order. Rodney meticulously cleaned and reset the trap we had once caught Dash in, while Shun spent her time studying our black slime samples, always searching for new insights, always trying to solve the puzzle.

As evening approached, we began preparing the night's meal. The responsibility rotated between us, each adding a personal touch to the simple, wild ingredients we had gathered. While one of us cooked, the others updated our shared journal, recording the day's observations, challenges, and victories.

After dinner, we usually spent an hour or two in open discussion, brainstorming, hypothesizing, and challenging each other's ideas about the black slime and our strange circumstances. Often, we pulled out the books we had brought, cross-referencing and fact-checking, trying to piece together the enigmatic puzzle before us. As night fell, we found ourselves beneath a blanket of stars, pondering the mysteries of Cognimyxa dominator until sleep finally claimed us. For me, that meant retreating to the research tent, alone with my swirling thoughts, only to wake at dawn and do it all over again.

I learned things about myself that I would have preferred not to know. *Why had I come to this place?* I found myself asking that question more and more. Curiosity had driven me to give up everything, to come here and witness what no human had ever seen. But now, in the thick of it, I realized how naive I had been.

I had been prepared to spend my life here—like some kind of Robinson Crusoe lost in time—but I had foolishly imagined a more idyllic existence. I understood the risks of living among dinosaurs in their natural habitat, of course, but I had underestimated the environment itself: the scorching sun, the relentless humidity, the massive storms, and the constant presence of unfamiliar insects. Even if I had been at full strength, this environment would still have taken its toll on me. My childhood dream had quickly become a nightmare. I missed my office at the university, and even the bitter coffee from the outdated machine in the hallway. I would have given anything to study prehistory from a book rather than live in it. But there seemed to be no hope of returning.

I usually kept these thoughts—these regrets—to myself, but my mood made it clear that I wasn't content. During one particularly fierce thunderstorm, with rain whipping my face from the strong winds, I finally snapped. Shun kindly asked me to bring some samples inside the tent so they wouldn't get ruined in the downpour.

"What's the point!" I yelled through the rain. "Huh, Shun, what's the point?"

"What do you mean?" she asked, startled.

"I mean... all this research!" A nearby lightning strike illuminated my gaunt, malnourished face. "Just why!" I stepped closer so she could hear me over the storm. "Who's going to read about our discoveries, huh? No one, that's who! Where are we going to publish our findings? This is insane. All our hard work will be forgotten!"

"That's why you came here? For recognition?"

I wiped the rain from my face, seething.

"Of course not, it's just that—" I stopped myself mid-sentence. She was wrong, but I couldn't explain why. It wasn't about validation, nor was it purely for the pursuit of knowledge. I had come here for her. I realized that now. "Just forget it!"

I picked up the samples and brought them inside the tent, then I collapsed, sobbing uncontrollably. It was as if a dam had finally broken, releasing all the emotions I'd been bottling up for so long. Each tear that rolled down my cheek seemed to carry with it memories, regrets, and unspoken confessions. *Why now? Why in this moment?* I had faced countless challenges and hardships up to this point, always maintaining a stoic front. But the weight of unsaid words, repressed feelings, and denied truths had finally become unbearable.

Shun sat down next to me and placed her hand on my shoulder. It was a bittersweet touch.

"It'll be alright," she said. "You just need time to acclimate to the climate here. It's been tough, especially with the rough start you had, but you'll get there."

I wanted to embrace her, but I wasn't sure how she'd react, so I just sat there, shivering like a pathetic schoolboy.

"I... I want to go home," I said between sobs. "I'm just so, so tired, you know?"

"You just need to adapt," she said gently. "There's still so much to figure out about this place." She paused, then looked at me with a hint of concern. "And... I have a feeling our research might be more important than you think."

"Is everything alright?" Rodney poked his head inside the tent, wearing one of his now surprisingly confident smiles. "I thought I heard yelling."

Shun let go of my shoulder, a little too quickly for it to feel natural, and smiled at Rodney in a way she had never smiled at me.

"No, we're alright," she said. "Aren't we, Ian?"

I nodded, though it didn't feel true.

After that night, everything continued as before. There was no sign that Shun's intuition about things turning out alright had any basis in reality. The storm passed, the merciless sun returned, and our routines continued unchanged. Meanwhile, my mental health kept spiraling downward.

I was hunched over our makeshift wash basin—a hollowed-out log lined with waterproof fabric—methodically scrubbing a pile of grimy clothes. With no real detergent, I'd resorted to using a paste of ash and water, rubbing it into the fabric before rinsing it with water from the stream. The process was tedious, but there was a certain satisfaction in bringing the clothes back to some semblance of cleanliness.

My hands were coated in gray sludge, the sharp smell of ash hanging in the air, when Rodney emerged from the treeline. His usually calm face was tight with concern, and he wasted no time getting my attention.

"There's someone yelling in the forest," he said, his words sending an immediate knot of tension through my stomach.

"What do you mean?" I asked, pausing my laundering and wiping my hands on the nearby grass. "A human voice?"

"Yes," he replied, a crease forming between his eyebrows. "It sounds like one, but I can't make out what they're saying."

We quickly retrieved Shun from the research tent and took up a position on the cliff where Rodney had heard the cries, overlooking the looming black mountain with its jagged spires.

"Are you sure it wasn't just an animal? Some animals can sound almost human, like foxes or marmosets," I asked.

"I can't be completely certain," Rodney admitted.

We stood in silence, straining our ears for any hint of the sound. "What exactly did it sound like?" I asked. Before Rodney could answer, a faint echo rose from the forest below.

"There!" Rodney exclaimed. "Did you hear that?"

"Yeah," Shun confirmed as the sound repeated. "It sounds like a woman."

"She can't be far," I speculated. "Otherwise, we wouldn't be able to hear her at all."

"What is she saying?" Rodney asked. "Can we make it out? It sounds like words, but at the same time—"

"Does it sound like Swedish?" Shun asked.

"No," Rodney replied, squinting through his binoculars, hoping to catch a glimpse of the person. "I suspect—"

"It must be one of the other passengers," I interrupted excitedly. Shun was about to object, but I was too caught up in the thought of seeing another human being to notice. "Hello!" I yelled with all my strength, waving my arms. "We're here!"

"Are you out of your mind?" Shun hissed.

"What?" I asked, baffled. "We have to help—"

"We don't know who or what that is," she interrupted. "You might have just given away our position to—"

"You're not seriously suggesting that the slime can imitate human voices, are you?" I countered.

Shun narrowed her eyes at me. "If it can control other dinosaurs, isn't it conceivable that it could have taken control of some of the other passengers too? We've discussed this several times! What you just did was *incredibly* irresponsible, Ian."

I swallowed hard as her words sank in. I had been too exhausted, too burnt out, to think it through. "I'm sorry," I said.

"But what if it is a survivor? We'd never have found them down there—it's far too dangerous for us. Calling out was all we could've done."

"We could've used the drone," Shun said, her disappointment in me unmistakable. "We could've—"

"Guys," Rodney interrupted. "She's stopped shouting."

A chill ran down my spine.

"We'll stay here and listen a bit longer," Shun decided. "After that, we all need to keep watch until we feel safe again. Honestly, we might have to start considering moving the camp."

"If the organism heard us, it won't wait to make its move," Rodney pointed out. "Last time, it reacted within minutes of spotting us."

"I'll go pack the essentials, just in case we need to flee," Shun said with a heavy sigh. "What were you thinking, Ian?"

"This is what happens when you haven't slept properly for weeks," I said. "If I were healthy..." I trailed off, noticing Shun's disinterest in hearing my explanation. "As I said, I'm truly sorry. But what if it was a survivor? Should we send the drone to look for any traces?"

"There's no time for that now," Shun said. "We have to assume the worst and prioritize safety above everything else. Once we're certain it's safe, we can start thinking about searching for potential survivors down there."

"If we move the camp," Rodney interjected, "I recommend heading toward the coast. We'd have access to more diverse food sources—fish, shellfish, even seaweed—and the visibility would be better for spotting threats. Plus, there might be caves or cliffs to use as shelter, and fresh water flowing from streams or springs into the sea. It could give us a safer, more sustainable setup."

"That would be a long journey," Shun said, "maybe too long,

with too many risks along the way… But I agree, if we can reach the coast, it would probably be the best option."

That night, as we took turns patrolling the camp, our eyes vigilant for any signs of intruders, I found myself staring up at the starry sky. I couldn't help but wonder if the enigmatic life form had come from up there, from one of the unknown stars above—perhaps from a star that, for a brief moment in history, passed near our solar system. The thought was dizzying. Then, I saw something else in the sky. A dark spot, barely visible as it passed in front of the stars. My heart caught in my throat.

I rushed over to Shun, who was chatting with Rodney, sharing a laugh. I slowed down, as though something instinctual held me back. As I approached them, something felt off—not just because of my fatigue. Shun casually touched Rodney's arm as she turned toward me... and he didn't even flinch. A thought surfaced at the edge of my mind, a realization I hadn't considered before. I swallowed hard, pushing the unsettling notion aside, and continued toward them.

"L-Look up," I stammered, my jaw suddenly weak. "What on earth is that?"

The dark spot was still overhead, slowly drifting away. Rodney quickly grabbed his binoculars. "I can barely see anything," he said. "It's completely black."

Shun took the binoculars from him. "Let me see," she said. "There's... something hanging from it. Tentacles, I think."

"So, it's the slime mold," I said. "Damn it. It must've come looking for us."

"How can it stay airborne?" Rodney wondered aloud. "Gas? It has no wings."

"Maybe it hasn't seen us," I suggested. "We did extinguish the fire, after all."

"It can't be a coincidence that it's here now," Shun asserted.

A few hours before dawn, when exhaustion had taken over and I could no longer keep watch without risking missing something, I excused myself, saying I needed some sleep. Shun's expression hinted at mild displeasure. She probably thought I should've stayed up to let them rest, given that it was my mistake that had put us in this position in the first place, but even so, she didn't object. Instead, she simply said I could take over when she or Rodney needed a break in a few hours.

I wasn't just exhausted—I felt like my heart had sunk into my stomach. The memory of the touch between them had lodged itself in my mind, and no matter how hard I tried to think of something else, it kept resurfacing. Lying on my back in the tent, it completely consumed me, stealing any hope of sleep.

How could I have been so blind? I thought of Rodney's transformation—from an overweight loner with no social skills to a muscular survivor thriving in the wilderness. Meanwhile, I had taken the opposite path. Anxiety surged in my chest, and I clenched my teeth hard, trying to suppress the thoughts. *What had they been up to during the nights since I'd moved to the research tent?*

I couldn't stop the images of them in each other's arms, deliberately silent so I'd remain oblivious while I lay there, dreaming of turning my life around and becoming the man I once was—a man who could provide Shun with a sense of security. Along with these intrusive thoughts came a surge of anger, directed at Rodney, as if he had taken something from me that wasn't his to take. I knew, intellectually, how childish my reaction was—Shun was a person, not an object one could claim or have "first dibs" on. I couldn't reasonably be upset that Rodney had accepted her desire to be with him. It was their business, and it had nothing to do with me. They didn't need my permission. I knew it, but my feelings didn't care for reason in that moment. Exhausted and sleep deprived, I tossed and turned on the sleeping pad, sweating profusely as jealousy, anger, and grief consumed me—my mind fixated on the thought of them alone in the tent at night. I imagined Shun gently touching him, tenderly and slowly, over weeks perhaps, easing him into her touch until it escalated to… My thoughts were abruptly shattered by the sound of a gunshot. I shot up from the sleeping pad and rushed outside, still only in my underwear.

"What's going on?" I asked.

Shun and Rodney were firing at something on the ground, their faces tense, illuminated by the rapid flashes from their submachine guns.

"Get the flashlight!" Shun yelled. "Now, Ian!"

I sprinted to the charging station by the research tent, grabbed a flashlight, and aimed the beam at the ground. The sharp smell of gunpowder filled the air, reminiscent of civilization. They had killed a giant snake, white and partially covered in the black slime, that had slithered its way up the hill.

"What does this mean?" I asked. "Has it found us?"

"I don't know," Shun replied. "Probably."

"But it's dead," I said. "It can't return to report—"

"If it doesn't return, more might be sent out," Shun interrupted, "and that flying organism has likely already informed the swarm of our location."

"It's just an animal," I insisted. "I get that it's clever, but it can't possibly think strategically like—"

"Don't touch me!" It was Rodney. "Help!"

I swung the flashlight toward him, and my heart nearly stopped at the sight. Two figures had grabbed hold of Rodney. Shun raised her gun but hesitated—she couldn't get a clear shot.

"Hey!" she yelled. "Let him go!"

They were as pale as the other infected creatures we'd encountered, but these were human. Moving with unnerving speed, they dragged Rodney down toward the jungle as he continued to scream for help. The black patches on their naked bodies glowed faintly blue in the darkness.

"It must've taken control of the other passengers," I said, disbelief washing over me. "Just like you suggested."

Shun, on the verge of a panic attack, stood motionless for a moment, as if desperately trying to solve an impossible mystery in seconds. Then, she bolted off to save Rodney. I dashed into the tent, grabbing extra ammunition and one of the guns, and took off after her—still in my underwear. Shun was already too far ahead to reach, but I still stumbled down the hill, naively hoping to catch up. Branches scratched my face, and sharp rocks cut into my feet as I ran. Somewhere in the darkness ahead, Shun's gunfire echoed.

"Where are you?" I yelled.

I kept running until, out of nowhere, she grabbed my arm, stopping me in my tracks. Just a hundred meters ahead, the creature we had seen in the sky had landed in a glade, surrounded by a swarm of smaller beasts—creatures unlike any dinosaurs we'd ever encountered, if they could even be called that. The infected humans were carrying a struggling Rodney through a large orifice in the creature's body. Resembling an organic blimp covered in blisters and tendrils, the giant being soon ascended into the air, while the other creatures swarmed below, their bodies glowing in the darkness.

Horrified, I raised my gun, but Shun pressed down on the barrel with her trembling hand.

"No," she said. "If you shoot, it'll ignite the gas inside its bladder, causing an explosion that could kill not just Rodney, but all three of us."

"They took him," I whispered. "We need to hide!"

Shun cursed, tears welling up in her eyes as she watched the airborne abomination drift away. Leaning forward with her hands on her knees, her voice shook as she cried, "Rodney, Rodney, Rodney… I'm sorry… I'm so sorry…"

"Let's go!" I urged. "We need to get the hell out of here before those… things catch our scent."

Defeated, we retreated to the lookout where we spent the night, our fingers resting on the triggers of our guns, ready for anything. We didn't speak for a long time. I sat in my corner, and she sat in hers. Still undressed, I was freezing, but Shun trembled even more than I did. Then, suddenly, she spoke, as if beside herself:

"He was our responsibility, Ian! We failed him. I should've kept my eyes on him."

"There was nothing we could've done," I tried to reassure her. "We couldn't have predicted—"

"Yes, we could! And we did! We should never have brought him here." She stood up and began pacing back and forth on the small platform, avoiding my gaze.

"He chose to come, Shun. He was an adult."

"You know he had special needs. He wasn't—" She paused, looking down in shame before finally meeting my eyes. "We have to save him."

"What do you mean, save him?" I asked, incredulous. "They probably took him to the nest. We can't go there—it's too dangerous."

"We can't just leave him behind!" she insisted.

She wasn't thinking clearly, which was understandable, given how upset she was.

"We'll see," I said gently, trying to comfort her. "Let's head back to camp tomorrow, in daylight, and gather what we need.

After that, we can talk about what to do next." I waited for her response, but she remained silent. "Okay?"

"Okay," she muttered, her tone edged with defiance.

The rest of the night was spent in silence, our ears tuned to the haunting sounds of the forest, sleep eluding us. At sunrise, we made our way back to camp. To our surprise, everything was untouched. Fat flies buzzed around the dead snake, which looked even larger in the daylight. The black slime on its body seemed to pulse, still creeping, still alive.

"Pack the essentials," Shun ordered, keeping her composure and masking the unease beneath. "Grab the plastic boxes, roll up the solar panels, and please, put some clothes on."

I quickly got dressed and followed her instructions, grabbing Dash in passing, who was skittering around in her cage, seemingly unfazed by everything that had happened.

"I'm going to take a sample of the slime," Shun continued, crouching over the snake.

"Why?" I asked, frowning. "We need to focus on surviving right now."

"Don't you get it?" she shot back. "That's exactly what I'm doing. I want to figure out how to kill this thing."

"Where are we going?" I asked, ignoring her remark.

"Back to the lookout," she replied. "We don't have time to set up a new camp. We'll have to do everything from there."

She was right. The platform was our safest option, but it was cramped, barely enough space for the two of us. It felt even smaller once I set up the plastic boxes to collect rainwater and unrolled the solar panels. From that day forward, life grew even more challenging.

Amidst the chaos and panic, Shun clung to her research like a lifeline, as if it were the one thing keeping her from spiraling into despair. It seemed she had funneled all her fears and anxieties into a singular goal—understanding Cognimyxa dominator. Her focus shifted abruptly, no longer centered on the rich tapestry of the land's ecology, but solely on unraveling the mystery of this strange organism. Shun dedicated a significant portion of each day to studying the slime mold samples we had collected. With her portable microscope in hand, she meticulously examined the mold's structure, searching for patterns or any potential weaknesses in its biological makeup. Her focus was intense, as though unlocking its secrets was the key to our survival.

Often, Shun would isolate different segments of the mold, subjecting them to various elements—heat, light, cold, and even the limited chemical substances we had in our makeshift lab. She was determined to find a reaction, a weakness in the mold's otherwise impenetrable defenses. Over time, her fingers became stained with the black residue, a persistent reminder of her relentless pursuit to unlock its secrets.

In the meantime, the responsibility of survival fell squarely on my shoulders. The forest, with its towering trees and cascading waterfalls, proved to be an unforgiving taskmaster, presenting fresh challenges every day. My main priority was keeping us nourished, and although it wasn't ideal, the abundance of insects in the canopy became a reliable source of protein.

Armed with a net and a sturdy stick, I ventured out each morning in the soft light of dawn, combing through dew-kissed leaves to catch beetles, grubs, and other critters. Though the disgust remained, it had dulled with time, worn down by the force of routine. The steady hum of insects became my constant soundtrack, a kind of white noise that helped mask the ever-present dread and the vigilance required to survive.

Fishing was another responsibility that fell to me. Instead of digging for worms on the forest floor, which I preferred to avoid, I baited the hooks with chunks of fruit or the entrails of insects. Each time I felt the line tug and a fish bit, it was a small but much-needed victory.

Water remained as crucial as ever for our survival, with the nearby stream serving as our lifeline, supplemented occasionally by rainwater. Every few days, I would make the trek to refill our empty containers. The routine had become almost meditative—wading into the cold stream, feeling the icy water seep through my clothes, and listening to the soothing sound of the current burbling around me. In those moments, the weight of fear and uncertainty seemed to lift, offering a brief but welcome escape from the constant dread hanging over us.

At the end of each day, I would try my hand at preparing our meager meals. Cooking had become a delicate balancing act—we needed enough heat to cook the food, but we couldn't risk a fire that might attract the attention of the slime mold or, even worse, ignite a wildfire. I constructed a small stone hearth, tucked beneath dense foliage to keep it concealed. There, I carefully grilled the fish and roasted the bugs over small, controlled flames, trying to make the most of what little we had while keeping us safe.

All the while, Shun remained focused on her research, her tenacity unshaken. I often caught glimpses of her, hunched over her samples, a look of intense focus etched on her face. She kept clinging to her purpose—studying the slime—with an obsessive zeal, showing no signs of giving up.

Although we lived in such close quarters, we drifted further apart with each passing day. We only spoke when absolutely necessary. She focused on her tasks, and I focused on mine. It took all this time for me to finally accept that she never loved me—and never would. Occasionally, she shared her research progress, but it was difficult for me to fully grasp what she was doing. Day after day, she spent hours collecting plants, fruits, roots—anything she could find—and exposing the slime to them. This routine continued for weeks.

I was teetering on the edge of despair, but I kept my worries to myself, not wanting to strain the already tense silence between us. Then one evening, everything came crashing down. I stood by the lake, attempting to retrieve my fishing rod after a large creature had yanked it from my grip, pulling it into the water and snapping the line. It was reckless to be out there alone, even with a firearm at my side, but I couldn't take it anymore. The weight of isolation, frustration, and the ever-present danger pressed heavily on me, and I needed a distraction—something, anything, to keep me from breaking.

Shun could have helped me if I had asked, but I hadn't. I couldn't bear the thought of her cold, antagonistic tone, the underlying hostility that seemed to color every word she spoke. Instead, I stubbornly struggled alone, using a stick to try and fish the rod out of the water.

"What are you doing?" Shun called from the lookout. She had been too absorbed in her work to notice my absence until now. "Don't be reckless! The rod will drift ashore soon enough—you don't need to risk it!"

I looked up at her, frustration boiling over. "We need food! I haven't eaten in two days!" I snapped.

Her eyes widened with alarm. "Ian, listen carefully. Don't look behind you—just do as I say, okay? Slowly walk toward the tree and climb it. Now."

A shiver ran down my spine. Despite her warning, I couldn't resist the urge and turned around. Emerging from the water was a terrifying lizard-like creature, as big as an alligator, from a species I couldn't have identified even if I tried.

The other half of my fishing line dangled from its drooling jaws. It huffed and puffed, taking slow, deliberate steps toward me before unleashing a deafening roar. Paralyzed by fear, I could feel its rancid, warm breath wash over my face. Then, instinct kicked in, and I bolted. As the creature lunged after me, I slipped, crashing into a puddle of mud.

"Get up!" Shun shouted, panic rising as she waved her arms and made loud noises to distract the creature, which, to her dismay, paid her no attention.

I lay on my back, frozen, as the creature prepared to pounce, its claws poised to strike. Desperation surged through me as I aimed my weapon and fired, my weak arms struggling to control the recoil. I missed, but the thunderous blasts startled the creature, making it flinch just long enough for me to scramble to my feet.

Shun reached out, gripping my arm as I struggled to find my footing against the tree trunk. I clambered up toward the platform, the creature lunging and snapping its jaws just below my feet. With a strong, decisive pull, she hauled me the final distance. I collapsed onto the platform, tumbling into her, but she quickly shoved me aside.

"Such reckless behavior!" she snapped. "You could've at least told me before running off like that!"

"What for!" I shot back. "Would you have even listened? You didn't even notice I was gone! We can't keep going like this, Shun. Can't you see that?"

"If it wasn't for your—"

"I've already said I'm sorry!" I interrupted, my words spilling out before she could finish.

"Prove that you mean it," Shun said, wiping a tear from her eye. "You can't just say you're sorry and expect everything to magically get better. You, of all people, should be the most invested in saving Rodney, considering it was your—" She stopped, clearly reluctant to finish the thought I knew she was holding back: that Rodney's abduction was my fault. She sighed deeply. "But you don't care, do you? You just... don't seem to care at all."

"Of course I care," I said, my voice rising. "But try to be realistic for once. That creature—that damn slime mold—it doesn't take prisoners. Don't you get it? It's too late." I hesitated, knowing I shouldn't say the next part but unable to stop myself. "Rodney is dead, Shun."

"You don't know that!" she exclaimed, her voice cracking as tears streamed down her cheeks. "He might be infected. And if that's the case, there could be a cure! That's what I'm spending every single day trying to figure out."

"Listen," I began, my expression softening. "I understand how you feel... What happened to Rodney is horrific. I think about him every day. I blame myself for what happened, just like you do. But if we want to survive—if we ever hope to take revenge on that thing in the black mountain—we have to start thinking long-term. We need to move on." I paused, hoping my words would sink in. "We need to go back to our old camp, gather whatever supplies we can, and find a new, safer place to set up camp. Somewhere along the coast, just like Rodney suggested," I continued. "For God's sake, Shun... What do you think Rodney would have wanted? He wouldn't want us to die here too, right? He would want us to survive, to keep going."

Shun's lower lip quivered. "You understand nothing," she said. "Rodney wouldn't have abandoned us. He would have fixated on finding a solution, no matter how impossible it seemed. But you… you just want to move on, leave everything behind, and pretend that we could somehow live together in some harmonious paradise. But that will never happen, Ian. Never!" Her eyes hardened. "So, you have a choice: survive on your own, or help me find a way to save Rodney."

Her words felt like a punch to the gut. The weight of that single "never" hung in the air with unmistakable finality. It was clear—there was no going back, no mending what had been broken. For a brief moment, I considered her advice: leaving her behind, heading to the coast, and carving out a solitary existence. But I couldn't. Despite everything, I still cared for her. And the truth was, she wouldn't survive without my help.

"As you wish," I said quietly. "But sooner or later, you'll have to accept that Rodney isn't coming back."

As time passed, the light of hope in Shun's eyes began to fade, hinting at a quiet resignation brewing beneath the surface. Yet, just days after she started showing signs of giving up, something unexpected happened—something I now deeply wish had never occurred. Her relentless dedication to experimentation had finally paid off. She had made a groundbreaking discovery in biochemistry: an innovative myxomycete-inhibitor ointment.

"It works!" Shun exclaimed, her words shaking with the first sign of excitement in weeks. She was nearly in tears from the relief. "My God, Ian, it works!"

I closed my eyes, feeling a wave of despair wash over me—long enough for Shun to notice I didn't share her exhilaration. This discovery could only mean one thing: she would now venture out to the black mountain, clinging to the impossible hope of saving Rodney.

"It... it really works?" I said, dreading the answer.

"Yes, Ian—and it's all thanks to you!" Shun said, her eyes gleaming with excitement.

"Wait, what?" I stammered, confused. I searched her face for any sign of a joke. "What do you mean?"

“Hear me out,” she said, her excitement seemingly making her forget her resentment toward me. “This ointment is a blend of several key ingredients—the most important being formic acid. It’s a simple carboxylic acid found in nature, especially in the stings and bites of certain insects. If it hadn’t been for your encounter with those bugs back when we first set up camp, and if we hadn’t followed your advice to kill them instead of just moving them—like I originally suggested—I wouldn’t have discovered its effect on the slime. Thanks to you, I had thousands of those bugs in storage to use for my experiments!”

I chuckled at the irony. “That’s—That’s great.”

“It’s more than just the formic acid, though,” Shun continued, her excitement growing. “There are two other crucial components: fruit extracts and a specific flower extract. The fruit extract, aside from its pleasant fragrance and taste, has strong antimicrobial properties. As for the flower extract, I obtained it through a delicate process of steam distillation. This yielded an essence rich in phytochemicals—powerful compounds known for their therapeutic effects and protection against various pathogens. This ointment is the result of countless iterations, delicate adjustments, and methodical testing. Rodney would—no, will—be proud!” She smiled for the first time in what felt like forever. “The formic acid had to be carefully neutralized to ensure it was safe for human skin contact—I didn’t want to risk subjecting us to the same horrible reaction you had earlier. And the fruit and flower extracts needed to be purified and concentrated to enhance their bioactive properties. After balancing these three components with precision, I’ve finally created a cream that works as a strong myxomycete inhibitor. Ian… this ointment doesn’t just repel the black slime. In high enough concentrations, it could actually eradicate it. This is a revolutionary breakthrough in our fight against the slime mold!

It's possible we could remove the infestation from the host if we administer a strong enough dose of the cream. Do you understand what this means? We can save Rodney!"

"That's more than you've said to me in weeks," I replied, with a hint of bitterness. "But I'm glad to see your old self again. Really, I am."

"I'm going to make a lot of this," she continued. "It won't harm us—at least, I don't think it will."

"H-Harm us?" I said, feeling a knot form in my stomach. "What exactly do you plan to accomplish?"

"What do you think?" she said, her eyes lighting up. "We'll cover ourselves in this ointment to protect us from the slime mold, then coat our clothes in the slime itself for camouflage. That way, we can sneak inside the nest and save the others."

"I see…" I said, horrified by the very idea. "But, Shun…" I hesitated, not wanting to ruin the rare flicker of hope in her eyes. "What makes you think they're even still alive?" I sighed, searching for a gentler way to express my concerns. "It's incredible that we have this treatment now... Honestly, what you've achieved is astonishing. But you have to let go of this obsess—" I stopped myself, realizing my words weren't getting through. "Look," I continued, "this discovery of yours will keep us safe, protect us. But the others? They're gone, Shun."

"They might be infected right now," she said, "but if they ingest this substance, it will kill the slime and free them from its control."

"No," I replied, shaking my head. "After all this time... there's nothing left, Shun. We have to face that."

"Please!" she pleaded, her desperation breaking through. "Just consider the alternative for a second, would you?"

"What alternative?" I asked, uncertain where she was going with this.

"We're just two people," she said. "You and me. What if something happens to me? You're not equipped to survive here alone. It's unlikely we'll make it if it's just the two of us. Remember, we're talking about the rest of our lives here."

"What are you trying to say?" I asked, my voice quiet, unsure of her direction.

"Our only hope for long-term survival is to save the others," she explained, her eyes intense. "If we do that, we can establish our own tribe—our own society, if you will. We're human beings, Ian. We need a pack to survive, to function."

"I hate you," I said, lowering my head to hide the defeat that washed over me.

"Ian, please…" she began.

"I hate you… because you're right."

A small smile crept onto her face, but instead of bringing me comfort, it filled me with dread.

Shun worked tirelessly, producing more of the cream, while I took on the daily tasks to keep us going—this time with a little less resentment, given that we were finally on speaking terms again, even if things were still far from friendly. But maybe, I thought, there was a chance we'd find our way back to that too—especially if we somehow managed to save Rodney. The thought that everything could return to normal if we saved him gave me a sliver of hope, even against these impossible odds, motivating me to push myself harder than I thought possible. Still, I couldn't shake the unease about how we planned to execute the mission. The idea of covering myself with that cream—the very substance that had sparked my misery in this place—sent a shudder down my spine. But it seemed there was no alternative.

"We need to test our plan," Shun said late one night. "I suggest we cover Dash in the slime and let her loose near the base of the black mountain, preferably under one of those sacks of eyes. If our theory holds, nothing will happen to her, and she'll run off to freedom."

"You want to use Dash?" I stammered, feeling a knot tighten in my chest. "I-I don't think that's a good idea. She's kept us safe... and, honestly, I've grown attached to her."

"It would take too long to capture another one," Shun said with a sigh. "I wish we didn't have to, but it's our only option as far as I can see."

"What happened to not killing any mammals?" I countered. Then, after a moment of thought, I added, "Why don't we use fish instead? We could catch a few and throw them to an infected animal. That would allow us to test how it reacts to fish without the slime and others covered in it. This way, we wouldn't have to risk Dash's life."

Shun nodded thoughtfully. "That might work. Will you catch the fish, then?"

"With pleasure," I replied.

The next day was spent with my fishing rod in hand, patiently catching several fish, which I kept alive in one of our plastic containers. They weren't very large, but they were aggressive enough that I was confident they would catch the attention of whatever organism we threw them at.

Later in the day, while we ate in the usual silence, Shun stood up and grabbed Dash's cage, surprising me by sitting down next to me. For a moment, she simply watched as Dash scurried across the cage floor. Then, she finally spoke.

"It's time to release her," she said. I swallowed hard, understanding the grim reality behind her suggestion. "We don't know when, or if, we'll be back. It wouldn't be right to risk her starving to death in the cage."

I nodded silently, my eyes fixed on Dash. After we finished our meager meal, we climbed down from the platform and carried the cage to a cluster of bushes that would offer some protection. There, we opened the cage. Dash hesitated for a moment, as if sensing a trap, but eventually stepped out, leaving the safety of the cage behind.

"Go on, friend," I said. "Soon, this world will be yours."

With that, she darted off and vanished into the underbrush, leaving me with a hollow feeling.

As night fell, cloaking us in the relative safety of darkness, we ventured warily into the forest near the black mountain, ready to test our plan.

Shun moved swiftly through the forest, armed and focused, while I stumbled behind her, struggling with the container. The erratic movement of the fish inside caused the weight to shift constantly, making it difficult to maintain balance. Several times, I had to swerve to the left and right to keep the water from sloshing over the sides, my heart pounding in my chest like a trapped bird. Fear gripped me—not just from what might be lurking in the shadows, but also from the unpredictable fish threatening to leap out.

"Hey," I whispered, struggling to catch my breath. "Can you slow down a bit?" Shun turned around, irritation clear on her face. "I can't keep up with you carrying these damn fish," I added.

"You're the one who insisted on using the fish," she hissed. "Now try not to slow us down too much!"

My heart sank as the reality set in that there was a long road ahead before any kind of friendship between us could be rebuilt. We trudged on in tense silence. After what felt like endless kilometers, we finally reached an area of the forest where the black slime was visibly thick, coating the ground and trees.

Shun stopped abruptly, her finger resting on the trigger of her rifle, scanning the surroundings.

"We need to go left," Shun said. "I'm worried we'll be detected if we step on the slime. Let's stick to its perimeter and keep moving until we find one of those hanging eyes—or anything else we can throw the fish at."

As Shun suggested, we veered left. The ground was littered with bones and half-rotten carcasses, crunching under our boots, and the stench of decay hung thick in the air. My arms were growing weaker with every step, despite setting the container down several times to rest. I wasn't sure how much longer I could keep going. Just as I felt myself about to stumble forward, ready to spill the fish all over the ground, Shun turned to me and whispered urgently,

"Get down. There's an infected T-rex up ahead."

A cold shiver ran down my spine at her words. A Tyrannosaurus rex that close would catch us in a heartbeat if we were spotted. We wouldn't even have time to climb a tree. I held my breath, crouching as low as I could, following Shun's lead.

"Oh my God, oh my God, oh my God," I whispered. "What... what are we going to do?"

"It's just standing there," Shun replied, puzzled. "Look at it—it's so weird. It's almost as if..."

"What?" I demanded. "You know how fast they run—we need to get out of here, now!"

"Calm down," Shun whispered firmly. "We'll hide behind that fallen tree over there and throw the fish at it."

I stared at the old tree trunk, rooted to the spot. "Can't we find something less dangerous to throw the fish at?" I asked.

"We'll be careful." Shun had already started sneaking toward the trunk, leaving me no choice but to follow. I wasn't about to be left alone out here. "If we overstay our welcome, something else will find us," she added over her shoulder.

Reluctantly, I followed her, trying to steady my breath as we crept toward the tree.

Hidden behind the tree, I carefully set the container down. The fish inside thrashed about, their scales gleaming faintly under the moonlight.

"Let's cover one of them with the slime," Shun whispered, pulling out a plastic bag filled with the black substance she'd collected earlier. "We'll see how it reacts."

I quickly reached into the container, grabbing a fish that wriggled violently in my grip, nearly biting me as I fought to keep it still. Shun, focused and steady, began smearing the slime over the fish's body, meticulously ensuring it was almost entirely coated. The black substance clung to the fish like a second skin, the once gleaming scales now dull and slick.

"There," Shun whispered. "Make sure to throw it as close to the T-rex as possible."

I slowly peeked over the trunk, my heart pounding in my throat as I caught sight of the pallid Tyrannosaurus rex. Its left eye was shrouded in the black slime, and its pale, translucent skin looked inflamed and scabbed. The sight of its decaying, infected body sent a chill down my spine.

With a deep breath, I leaned forward, my arm pulling back, gripping the slimy fish tightly. This was it. I had to make the throw count. The Tyrannosaurus rex's head shifted slightly, its nostrils flaring as it detected the scent of something nearby. I seized up, my mind racing through every possible outcome, each more terrifying than the last. But I couldn't afford to hesitate. In one swift motion, I hurled the fish toward the massive predator. It landed just a few meters from its feet, wriggling feebly in the slime.

The Tyrannosaurus rex lowered its massive head, its singular, clouded eye locking onto the fish. Time seemed to slow, the tension hanging thick in the air as we held our breaths, waiting for its next move. And then, to our immense relief, it turned away, choosing to ignore the fish entirely.

"That's a good sign," Shun whispered. "Now let's try one without the slime. If it eats it, we'll know for sure."

I reached into the container for another fish, but before I could react, it clamped down hard on my hand with its sharp teeth. I bit back a scream as pain shot up my arm, intensifying with each second I kept silent. I yanked my arm out of the water, but the fish was still latched onto my hand, its body thrashing wildly, refusing to let go.

"Get it off," I whispered urgently, trying to contain my panic. "Get it off, get it off, get it off!"

Shun hushed me as she wrestled the fish off my hand, prying its jaws open with her fingers. The moment she freed me, blood started to pour from the bite mark, and throbbing pain shot up my arm. I could think of nothing else—my surroundings fading into a blur—until a rustling sound came from where the Tyrannosaurus rex had been standing idle. An icy shiver coursed through me, dulling the pain almost instantly. We both stopped in our tracks, our breath catching in our throats, bracing ourselves for what might come next. Shun cautiously lifted her head above the trunk to see what was happening, still clutching the fish.

"It's walking our way," she whispered. "It might have caught the scent of your blood. We have to move quickly." Without a second thought, she lobbed the fish toward the approaching creature. This time, the Tyrannosaurus rex didn't hesitate—it snapped up the fish in one swift motion. "It works," Shun said, her voice tinged with both relief and urgency.

"Th-that's great," I said, though part of me had secretly hoped her plan would fail. "Now what? How do we get out of here?"

The massive predator kept advancing, each heavy step bringing it closer to our hiding spot.

Shun quickly reached for the last fish in the container. "I'll try to distract it," she whispered. "Then we'll sneak away. Rinse your bloody hand in the water for a few seconds—it might confuse its sense of smell."

I did as she instructed, submerging my hand in the water, the cold sting biting at the wound. As soon as I pulled my hand out, Shun hurled the fish to our right, and we began retreating, carefully sneaking backward, praying that the diversion would work.

The Tyrannosaurus rex charged toward the fish, momentarily distracted as it scooped it up and swallowed it whole. For a brief moment, I thought our plan had worked, that we'd successfully diverted its attention. But then it let out a deafening grunt that echoed through the forest, shattering any sense of relief. The ground trembled beneath its massive weight as it turned its head back in our direction, nostrils flaring as it tried to pick up our scent once more.

The black goo covering its right eye seemed to hinder its vision, but its other senses were as sharp as ever.

"We need to run," Shun whispered urgently, her eyes wide with fear. "Now!"

Without waiting for a response, she bolted into the dense forest, and I followed right behind her. The underbrush crunched beneath our feet, and branches whipped against our faces as we sprinted through the trees. Behind us, the Tyrannosaurus rex's thunderous footsteps closed in, its grunts echoing through the forest, sending pterosaurs scattering in every direction.

My lungs burned, and my legs felt like they were made of lead, but the terror of the Tyrannosaurus rex closing in kept me moving. Each time I glanced back, I saw its massive form tearing through the trees, jaws snapping at the air, hungry for a kill. It was closing the gap, its hot breath mixing with the cold night air, creating a misty veil of death around its gaping maw. Shun, now running beside me, pulled out her rifle, her eyes sharp with focus despite the terror we both surely felt.

"Keep running!" she shouted as she turned and fired a few shots at the Tyrannosaurus rex. One bullet struck its left eye—the eye free from the black goo—and the creature roared in agony, lashing out wildly in response. But it didn't stop. Blinded and furious, our assailant barreled forward, its movements more chaotic yet no less relentless. I could feel its presence closing in, the raw power of its massive form bearing down on us. We were running out of time, and I knew it.

Then, by a stroke of luck, the Tyrannosaurus rex slammed into a massive tree with such force that the tree toppled over, crashing to the ground with a deafening boom. The forest reverberated with the noise, and for a brief moment, everything fell silent.

I turned, gasping for breath, and saw the colossal predator lying motionless, its body trapped beneath the fallen tree. Its chest heaved with labored breaths, each one weaker than the last, until, finally, it stopped moving altogether. The once formidable creature now lay still, its reign of terror over—felled by a single bullet. Shun and I stood there, our bodies trembling, adrenaline still surging through our veins. "You… you did it," I gasped. "You just killed a T-rex… literally." We stared at each other, the enormity of what had just happened sinking in, our hearts pounding in sync with the stillness of the night.

Shun nodded, her face pale but her eyes steely with resolve. "We survived," she said quietly. "But we need to move before reinforcements come." I stood there, still locked in place, staring at the fallen giant in disbelief. "Now, Ian!" she urged, snapping me out of my daze.

Without another word, we hurried through the dense forest, leaving the giant hunter behind, its translucent skin glowing faintly under the moonlight.

Since we couldn't conduct any reconnaissance inside the nest, we'd have to rely entirely on improvisation once we entered. I didn't have much hope for our survival, but without trying, there wouldn't be any hope for the future at all. We needed the others if we were going to have any chance of staying alive. Shun had been right about that.

She managed to compress her treatment into small pellets, which we intended to give to any survivors we might find. The next evening, I watched as she smeared her body with the ointment, her movements determined. Eventually, after covering all the parts of herself she could reach, she asked me for help. I stood up and moved behind her, nervousness causing saliva to accumulate in my mouth, forcing me to gulp.

As I applied the ointment to Shun's bare skin, a wave of dread surged through me—almost stronger than my fear of the mission itself. Touching her felt wrong, deeply uncomfortable, especially considering how she seemed to view me now. I was terrified of what she might be thinking, of the disgust she could be silently suppressing, as I watched my hands move awkwardly over her body. Then came the unwanted, repulsive surge of arousal—a yearning for physical intimacy so intense it nearly overwhelmed me. My hands, slick with the ointment, touched parts of her body she would never have allowed me to touch under any other circumstances. I tried to work quickly, avoiding lingering, yet I knew I couldn't let these feelings make me rush—our lives depended on my thoroughness. Once she was fully covered, I quickly stepped aside and undressed to apply the ointment to myself.

My hands trembled as I spread the cream over my skin, fear coursing through me. Even though the formic acid had been neutralized, it still burned, causing a painful tingling. It wasn't as intense as the sting from the insect bite, but it still hurt—like being wrapped in stinging nettles. Shun, now dressed in clothes she had treated with the slime before putting them on, stepped toward me and began assisting, just as I had helped her. The shameful pleasure of feeling her skin against mine returned, gnawing at the edges of my self-control and cutting through my better judgment. The discomfort of her touch far outweighed the physical irritation of the ointment on my skin. *What was she thinking as her hands moved over me?* I could only imagine that touching me now filled her with the same revulsion as handling the grotesque substance that had taken Rodney from her. Rodney... If we could somehow manage to save him—maybe, just maybe, things would return to normal, and Shun could finally forgive me.

When she finished, I carefully smeared my clothes with the slime we'd brought back from earlier expeditions—the thick, black substance oozing from the bucket. I then put on the clothes as slowly as possible, hoping to minimize the pain, but it didn't seem to make a difference.

"God, it burns," I said.

"It won't kill you," Shun replied, her tone offering no comfort.

"I've never been this uncomfortable in my entire life," I said, grimacing as I pulled my pants over my trembling legs. The fabric clung to my sticky, sensitive skin, intensifying the discomfort. With each garment that touched me, I squirmed, my body shivering as I clenched my jaws tight against the pain. It felt like the entire world was conspiring against me, punishing me for venturing where I didn't belong. I knew it was a ridiculous thought, but it lingered nonetheless.

Once we were both fully dressed in our slimy tactical suits, Shun strapped the grenade belt around her waist, slung a rifle over her shoulder, and handed me the second one. "Are you ready?" she asked.

"No," I replied honestly, "but there's no turning back now."

The sun was sinking below the horizon as we climbed down from the platform and ventured into the forest. Every step felt like walking through fire, the pain stiffening my body, but I had no choice. Shun couldn't do this alone. We pressed on.

As we emerged from the treeline into the valley, the vast expanse stretched before us, with the looming black mountain waiting on the other side. The stars above shone brightly, scattered across the sky like distant watchers.

"It's back!" Shun whispered, pointing upward. "Look!"

The comet was rising again, just as it had done a year and a half ago, its glow slowly ascending over the horizon.

"It only has an orbital period of about a year!" I exclaimed. "But that means—" I struggled to keep my burning neck from brushing against my collar. "I always thought it came from beyond Jupiter, but this means it must be an inner solar system object."

Shun didn't glance up. Her focus remained fixed on the landscape ahead, her gaze unwavering.

"We don't even know if it's the Chicxulub impactor," Shun said. "At this time, I'd assume the sky is filled with hundreds, if not thousands, of rocks."

As we crossed the valley, lit only by the ghostly green glow of the rising comet, a sense of impending doom crept over me. It was accompanied by a surreal feeling of inevitability—as if this was all meant to happen. But that disquieting calm didn't last. Terror quickly took over as I noticed three large shadows closing in on us. Their guttural, croaky grunts echoed through the night, leaving no room for doubt.

"Predators!" Shun yelled. "Big ones—Giganotosauruses, maybe T-rexes. Definitely large theropods. Run!"

They split up, trying to flank us from both sides.

"Where to?" I shouted. "They're too fast!"

I couldn't fathom how we'd escape them.

"The subway car!" she yelled back.

It wasn't until that moment I noticed its black silhouette looming in the darkness, about a hundred meters to our right. Our pursuers—uninfected, as far as I could tell—were closing in fast.

"Should I fire?" I called out.

"No," Shun urged. "We're almost there!"

"We're going to die, we're going to die, we're going to die," I panted, repeating the words over and over, my breath coming in ragged gasps.

"Don't look at them!" Shun shouted. "Don't look back!"

Just as the nearest theropod was about to reach us, we made it to the subway car. Without hesitation, Shun grabbed me and helped me scramble through one of the windows, pushing me inside just in time.

I collapsed onto the floor, quickly getting back on my feet to drag Shun in just moments before one of the theropods slammed into the side of the subway car. Its massive head poked through the window, drooling jaws grunting inches away from us. We crawled to the opposite side, raising our guns with trembling hands.

"Shoot it!" Shun screamed. "Shoot it!"

We opened fire, and the deafening sound of gunshots made the animal recoil, more frightened by the noise than by the bullets. As we stood, peering outside, we saw them circling the car, their hulking forms looming in the dark, unsure of their next move.

"We'll have to use one of the grenades," Shun said. "We need to scare them away."

"Won't that attract the attention of the swarm?" I asked.

"Hopefully, we'll have enough time to get out of the area."

Before I could protest, she pulled the pin and tossed the grenade. In one swift motion, she pushed me to the floor. A few seconds later, the explosion shook the subway car.

"It worked," Shun said, glancing out the window. "They're running away."

"But look," I said, my heart sinking as I pointed outside. "I told you! Look at the nest."

The bioluminescent Quetzalcoatlus, which had been circling the black mountain in the distance like glowing specters, shifted course and began flying directly toward us, their shimmering forms glittering ominously against the dark sky.

"Shit!" Shun exclaimed. "We need to run again. Now!"

It was impossible to tell exactly how much time we had before the Quetzalcoatlus reached us, but it was clear we didn't have long. With fear coursing through our veins and adrenaline driving us forward, we took off again—like prey fleeing from Mother Nature herself. Just as we neared the relative safety of the forest on the other side, about to enter the slime mold's mysterious domain, the enormous pterosaurs soared above us, their gigantic shadows sweeping over us like a dark omen as they passed, barely missing us.

Our plan had worked. Nothing seemed to notice us as we watchfully made our way toward the mountain. Our boots crunched softly on the shimmering slime coating the ground, breaking the otherwise haunting silence. The darkness ahead, illuminated by the faint luminescence within the ever-present slime, appeared almost peaceful in its alien beauty. Just a few meters ahead, an infected Triceratops lumbered forward at a slow, mechanical pace. I held my breath, every muscle tense. Here and there, crystal-like structures jutted out of the ground, adding to the surreal atmosphere.

"Why haven't we found any fossils of this organism?" I asked. "It seems like it's taken over large parts of the world."

"It doesn't have a bone structure or any easily recognizable patterns," Shun explained. "Chances are, we've come across traces of it but never identified them as anything significant. Those black crystals could be some form of cartilage or sugar, which wouldn't likely survive over millions of years. That's probably why nothing remains in the fossil record."

I had hoped our visit here would provide some answers, but the deeper we ventured into the territory, the more questions emerged. About a kilometer ahead, we entered a clearing and stumbled upon a bizarre biological structure. It was enormous—towering rib bones, likely from some massive creature, encircled a large mass of pulsating white flesh. The bones seemed to hold the grotesque form together. Atop the quivering mass, a single giant, unblinking eye stared skyward.

"What is this?" I whispered. "Shun, this... this is a structure, a *living* building."

She paused for a moment, her eyes locked on the grotesque scene before us. "Don't you get it?" she said quietly.

I was too terrified to even process what she might be thinking. "What are you saying?"

"It's an observatory," she continued. "This magnificent organism, this slime mold, it's not just some primitive life form like you thought."

"What's your theory?" I asked as we carefully sneaked past the enormous eye, trying to stay unnoticed.

She glanced at me, her expression serious. "I think it's sentient," she said. "It's *intelligent*."

"If it's really that intelligent, it should've taken over the entire planet by now," I said. "Just like humanity did in our time. Wasn't it you who said that once? That it was a mystery why it hasn't already done that?"

"Maybe," Shun replied. "I've had some thoughts on that, but let's see what else we discover first."

"K-Kira?" I stammered, my breath catching in my throat.

There she was, standing right in front of us—completely naked, her skin as pale as death itself. Black blotches marred her body, like ink stains spreading across her flesh.

"That's not Kira," Shun whispered.

"She's infected?" I whispered, panic rising in my chest. "But... her head was bitten off."

"That's not Kira," Shun repeated, backing away cautiously.

Before I could process her words, another figure jumped down from a nearby tree. Also Kira. They looked identical.

"What in heaven's name is going on?" I gasped, resisting the overwhelming urge to scratch the rashes spreading across my face due to the ointment.

Then a third stepped forward. And a fourth.

"It's found us," Shun said.

The pale figures in front of us let out a deafening, collective scream, baring their teeth like a pack of feral animals. Then they charged. Shun opened fire, and two of them dropped instantly, but just as quickly, two more emerged from the shadows to take their place. I fired too, but in the chaos, I couldn't tell if I'd hit anything.

Shun spun on her heel and bolted, shouting for me to follow. I quickly took off after her. To our left, I heard the heavy stomping of the Triceratops we had seen earlier. Our plan had failed. Every living thing—if you could even call them that—in the area had turned against us, acting as a single organism or perhaps a shared consciousness.

We had nowhere to run, yet we ran anyway. Several Quetzalcoatlus swooped down through the canopy, landing to our left, to our right, and directly in front of us. Shun skidded to a halt, unloading her rifle into one of the towering Quetzalcoatlus. Their long, terrifying necks loomed over us, wings spread wide as if to block our escape.

"Give me one of your grenades!" I shouted.

Without hesitation, she handed one over. I yanked the pin and hurled it at the infected versions of Kira, who were quickly closing in. The explosion momentarily confused the creatures, causing them to flinch, but they quickly refocused.

Shun was yelling something, but the roar of the blast had deafened me; her voice barely reached my ears, even though she was right beside me.

"—the cliff!" Shun shouted.

"What cliff?" I yelled back, struggling to hear over the chaos around us.

Before I could react, she grabbed my hand, pulling me along. Despite the surge of warmth that ran through me at her touch—a fleeting, naïve hope—it crashed hard against my better judgment as reality set in.

"We have to jump!" she cried.

I looked down. Twenty meters below, a river snaked its way toward the black mountain. There was no time to think, no room for hesitation. My feet felt cemented by fear, but Shun's grip tightened, refusing to let go. She yanked me forward, and together, we plunged into the abyss.

We were swept along by the violent current, struggling to stay afloat, our hands still clasped together. On either side, ghostly figures watched us—some vaguely human, others only human in shape. Their hollow eyes followed our every move, but we had no time to consider their presence.

The river funneled into a lava tube, its low ceiling forcing us beneath the surface. I felt Shun's hand slip from mine. Panic surged through me. *Where had she gone?* Everything was pitch black. I couldn't hold my breath much longer. Then, I was pulled down. An underground waterfall swallowed me whole, and I tumbled through the darkness. I let out a scream, but it was instantly drowned by the relentless surge of water as I fell, helpless, into the unknown depths below.

A sharp rock scraped against my arm, leaving a stinging gash. I tumbled down with the water until, finally, I hit the bottom of the fall and resurfaced. Gasping for air, I found myself in a much larger cave, where I could breathe again. The atmosphere felt lighter here, the oxygen levels lower—bringing some clarity to my mind, a clarity I hadn't experienced since arriving in this forsaken place. The blue glow of the slime illuminated the cavern walls, casting long shadows that danced with the flicker of the water.

"Shun!" I yelled, my voice echoing off the damp stone. "Where are you?"

The roar of the waterfall thundered beside me, drowning out nearly every other sound. Yet for a brief, terrifying moment, all I could hear was the rapid pounding of my own heart.

"Ian!" Shun's voice echoed through the cave. I spun around, searching frantically, and spotted her resurfacing a few meters away. An overwhelming sense of relief washed over me as I swam toward her. She smiled, the same relief reflected in her eyes. We were both alive.

"You're bleeding," she said, glancing at my arm.

"I-I know," I replied. "Everything hurts... and I'm freezing."

We pulled ourselves out of the icy water and collapsed onto the cold stone floor, too exhausted to care about the dampness soaking into our clothes. We sat in silence, catching our breath.

Around us, several cave openings glowed with the same blue light, casting an otherworldly glow in the darkness. Each tunnel seemed to beckon us deeper into the unknown.

"I think we're inside the nest," Shun whispered, her voice echoing faintly through the glowing cave. "Where's your gun?"

"Oh, crap," I said, patting my sides. "I must've lost it in the water."

"Same here. I've still got the grenades, though."

"And your repellent?" I asked, rubbing at the itching under my clothes. "It's still burning like hell under my shirt, so I guess it's still there. But the water probably washed it off my face."

Shun frowned. "I don't know. Let's hope we're still somewhat protected. At least the pellets for the others are intact. Hopefully, we can still use them to cure the infected."

My heart sank as the weight of our slim chances pressed down on me. "I don't want to die like this," I said, "or worse—become one of the slime's mindless drones."

Shun gave me a resigned look, her expression heavy with grim understanding. "I don't think any of those pale creatures we've seen are mindless drones," she said. "We're not dealing with a eusocial species, like an anthill where every member has a specialized task. This is just one organism—one mind—operating through all of them. I don't think it simply infects other organisms—or maybe it does, to some extent—but I believe it's doing something far more unprecedented. Something entirely unheard of in evolutionary history. It might hold the key to answering some of the questions that have been plaguing us all along."

"What are you talking about?" I asked.

"It's just speculation," she replied, rising to her feet. "But we don't have time to dwell on it. We need to either find the others or figure out a way out of here."

I stood up too, wincing as my body protested. "A way out

would be great," I said, hoping for anything that might lead us to safety.

We chose one of the caves at random, having no way to tell which path might lead us where we wanted to go. The air was thick with the stench of rotting meat, mingled with a sharp, ammonia-like odor. Hugging the cave wall, we moved stealthily, every corner a potential hiding place for something dangerous. Faint echoes of distant roars, grunts, and what sounded eerily like human screams reverberated through the tunnel, heightening our anxiety. The slime coated most of the walls, casting a dim glow that lit our way—though it also likely meant we were being watched.

The cave opened up to a natural bridge stretching over a vast chamber below. Beneath us, a pool of red goo bubbled ominously, and within it, two grotesque Tyrannosaurus rex appeared to be growing. Their translucent skin barely concealed the organs inside, as though they were unfinished—still forming.

"What in God's name—" I began.

"As I suspected," Shun said calmly.

"Excuse me?" I whispered as we crossed the bridge. "We're looking at two T-rexes being grown in what looks like a giant petri dish from hell, and you *suspected* this?"

"It's what I've been speculating, but I didn't dare draw any conclusions until now," Shun said, speaking steadily despite the horror below us. "This is a spawning pool. My first clue was the absence of spores. All known fungi reproduce via spores, and at first, it seemed logical to assume we were dealing with something similar. But when we realized it was a slime mold… things changed. Obviously, this isn't an ordinary slime—it's something far more complex. Every part of it behaves as though it's still connected, functioning as a single, unified organism."

"Yeah, but how does that explain—" I began, but Shun cut me off, her thoughts rushing ahead.

"And then there were the supposedly extinct dinosaurs," she continued. "That only reinforced my theory. The multiple versions of Kira made me almost certain, but this—this confirms it." She gestured toward the grotesque scene below. "Think about it: most organisms reproduce to pass on their genes before they die. The individual might perish, but the genetic material lives on in the offspring. Now imagine an organism that doesn't age—one that's biologically immortal. It wouldn't need to reproduce to preserve its genes. But such an organism would face a significant problem."

"And what's that?" I asked, still struggling to keep up.

"It can't adapt to a changing environment," Shun explained. "Over time, it would struggle to survive. But what if it found a way around that problem, either through evolution or its own intelligent design? Think about it. You were the one who suggested it first—an organism with intelligence comparable, maybe even superior, to our own should have been able to take over the entire planet. So why hasn't it?"

"I don't know," I admitted, still finding it hard to think clearly, even with the more manageable oxygen levels down here.

"I believe it's learned to acquire the genetic material of other organisms and then spawn them in these pools," Shun continued. "That's why we've seen those evolutionary older dinosaurs roaming around—it still remembers their genetic makeup. This organism must be ancient. And I don't just mean from our perspective. It must have been alive millions of years ago to retain genomes that old."

"But why?" I asked.

"That's the thing," Shun said. "I think it deliberately lets other species live, waiting for them to adapt to the environment so it can harvest their DNA and spawn versions of them for its own purposes. Who knows if this black slime mold is even its original form?"

"You're saying there could be some kind of immortal brain, somewhere on this planet, controlling all of this through some kind of network?"

"I know how it sounds, but just look around," Shun said. "I wish Rodney were here to contribute to these theories."

"And now this immortal organism has stolen our DNA too?" I asked. "That can't be a good thing."

The cave split into multiple paths, and once again, we chose one at random. That path, too, soon branched off in different directions—some leading downward, some continuing straight, and one sloping upward. Believing we were deep underground, we opted for the upward route. We repeated this process for hours, and with each passing hour, the cave seemed to narrow around us. Before long, we found ourselves crawling on our hands and knees just to keep moving forward.

I was utterly exhausted, my body aching with every movement as I shivered from the cold. The relentless itching beneath my clothes only worsened the discomfort as I crawled forward. I tried to picture home—warm showers, a glass of wine, curling up with a good book in the evening, lazy Saturday mornings in bed, safely pondering what a Tyrannosaurus rex might have looked like from the comfort of my own room. *Why had I ever come to this godforsaken place?* I wanted to cry, but before I could even muster the tears, my human emotions were once again overtaken by a primal, animalistic terror. Something hissed behind me, and though I couldn't turn my head to see it, I knew it had to be a giant snake—maybe a Titanoboa.

"Oh God, please, no," I whispered. "Please, I beg of you,

no." I wasn't even a religious man, but this was beyond what my rational mind could handle.

"Shun," I gasped, trying to pick up my pace despite the tight space. "I think there's an enormous snake behind me."

"What?"

"Just move faster!" I urged.

I was hyperventilating, my knees scraping against the uneven floor as I crawled frantically. The hissing grew louder, closer. I could now hear the slithering of its massive body against the ground.

"Can't you just give me a grenade and—" I started.

"No," Shun cut me off, "we'd die instantly."

I knew that, but panic had hijacked my thoughts.

"But it's going to swallow me whole any second now!"

"Don't think about it—just keep moving forward, as fast as you can."

"I can't go any faster! You have to—"

"What? I'm crawling as fast as—"

"Just go! Go, go, go!"

Shun squeezed through a narrow hole that led straight down, the only option after encountering rocks blocking our path. I followed her, even though the passage was impossibly tight. As I descended, the pressure dislocated my shoulder. A sharp jolt of pain shot through me, but there was no room to scream. Had I not been so unnaturally thin from malnutrition, I would have gotten stuck upside down in this claustrophobic tunnel. The mere thought of that fate was almost enough to distract me from the snake closing in behind. Almost.

Fortunately, the snake was too large to follow us into the narrow hole. It did manage to grab hold of my boot, but it slid off my foot just as I tumbled down into the chamber below. We landed in a pool of stagnant water, barely half a meter deep. As

I hit the bottom, a sharp pain shot through my left hand—I'd sprained it. I moaned in pain as Shun helped me to my feet. I felt utterly useless, more of a burden than a help at this point.

I struggled to move with only one boot, my bare foot either slipping on the slime or scraping against sharp rocks. The pain throbbing through my entire body slowed me down even further. Shun could have easily left me behind, but instead, she risked her life by coming back to help me. The cave system inside this mountain felt like an impossible maze. There were hundreds, if not thousands, of tunnels—either naturally formed or dug out by some creature—winding through the mountain. Suddenly, a group of cloned Thescelosaurus—ornithopod dinosaurs about as tall as a person—charged toward us from the right. Shun quickly pushed me behind her and grabbed a grenade. Before we could react further, Velociraptors burst in from another entrance, racing at full speed. Their distorted, high-pitched screeches merged into a sound that almost resembled twisted laughter. Shun didn't hesitate; she hurled the grenade toward the point where the Velociraptors and Thescelosaurus were converging.

The deafening ringing in my ears from the explosion drowned out all other sounds for what felt like forever. Knocked to the floor, I lay flat on my back, staring up at the ceiling of yet another tight crawl space, which seemed to shift and sway above me. Disoriented, it took me a moment to understand what was happening. Then it clicked—Shun was dragging me by my slime-covered jacket, pulling me through the tunnel.

We emerged into another small chamber, the floor covered in the same red water we had seen before—the same kind that had been growing the Tyrannosaurus rex. But here, to our horror, something far worse was taking shape beneath the surface. Human infants, in various stages of development, floated under the water, their fragile forms barely discernible in the murky glow.

At the center of the room, bathed in the pale blue light emanating from the walls, lay a figure stuck to a black crystal, held fast by slime. The dark substance writhed and crawled up toward his ears, slowly entering them. His eyes had been picked away, but even in that grotesque state, we recognized him instantly.

"Oh, no!" Shun gasped, tears welling in her eyes. "Oh, no, oh no, oh no."

It was Rodney. He was still breathing, but his body was so horrifically mutilated that saving him seemed impossible—perhaps even a fate worse than death.

"What in God's name has it done to him?" I whispered.

"We failed him," Shun choked out. "He trusted us to protect him. If only you hadn't—"

A wet, strained gurgle came from Rodney, cutting her off.

"He's trying to say something," I said. "Listen."

We leaned in, straining to catch whatever he was trying to say.

"...underground..." Rodney whispered hoarsely before stopping to vomit a thick, grey mucus. "...thermal energy storage..." His words became muffled, barely audible. "...Temporal..." More vomit, followed by a strained pause. "...crystal."

We stood there, waiting, hoping for something more coherent, but for the next ten minutes, nothing else came that we could understand.

"We have to go," I said, my voice filled with reluctant resignation. "There's nothing we can do for him."

Shun turned toward me, her eyes burning with rage—rage that felt more directed at me than the monstrous slime mold. "We can't leave him like this," she seethed.

Strange whispers began to emanate from the walls, faint at first, but growing in intensity. In the dim light, it was difficult to make out their source, but once our eyes adjusted, the sight became impossible to ignore. The walls were lined with naked bodies, each one suspended by the pervasive slime, their faces identical—each one bearing the face of Rodney. Their whispers sounded like robotic murmurs, cold and monotonous, as though they were running calculations. It was impossible to discern any actual words, if they were even using words at all. The sound was a mechanical hum, an eerie chorus of mindless processing.

"What is this?" Shun whispered. "What kind of nightmarish abomination—"

"I-I think it's using his brain," I stammered, "to create some kind of… computer. A human supercomputer, maybe."

Shun didn't respond. Her face hardened as she pulled out a grenade, quietly removing the pin and holding the safety lever.

"I'm so sorry," she said, her gaze locked on Rodney, her voice heavy with regret.

"Wait," I said.

"What?" Shun said, her face streaked with tears. "We can't leave him like this. I'll throw it, and then we'll run."

"I know," I replied, swallowing hard against the lump in my throat. "I just… I just wanted to say—" I paused, my discomfort swelling. "Y-you should put it in his mouth. The shockwave from the explosion will reach his brain faster than the nerve signals. He won't feel any pain… It'll be instant."

Shun's sobs became uncontrollable as she gently pressed the grenade into Rodney's drooling mouth, whispering through her tears, over and over, "I'm sorry, I'm sorry, I'm sorry." Blood-tinged tears trickled from Rodney's empty eye sockets, a silent acknowledgment of what was coming. Shun made sure the safety lever was released. "Come on," she said, pulling me toward the neighboring chamber.

We sat down with our backs against the cold stone wall, the entrance between us. I covered my ears, stealing a glance at her. Her face told me everything—she wasn't just mourning a friend. There was something deeper in her expression, something that went beyond grief.

"You loved him, didn't you?" I asked quietly.

Before she could respond, the grenade detonated. A rush of fire, rocks, and shredded flesh blasted into the chamber, passing right between us. She didn't need to say anything—I already knew.

As we left the cave, I wanted to comfort her, but she kept her distance, her silence creating an unspoken barrier. We didn't speak for a long time after Rodney's death. I hung back, giving her the space I thought she needed. But when she stopped abruptly in the middle of the cave, something in her stillness made me rush up to her without hesitation.

"Do you hear that?" she asked, barely above a whisper. "It's… *singing*."

At first, I hadn't noticed anything, but once she pointed it out, I caught the faint strains of what sounded like distant choral music, carrying a sacred, ethereal melody. The sound echoed from somewhere up ahead, growing clearer the closer we got. It was hauntingly beautiful, yet so eerily out of place in this nightmarish landscape that it unsettled me even more than the threatening grunts of the Tyrannosaurus rex.

"It's close," Shun whispered. "We'll be there soon."

"Beware of the siren call," I warned, though she didn't slow her pace.

We stepped into a massive chamber with a towering ceiling. The pulsating blue light seemed to sync with the ominous melody, casting ghostly shadows that danced across the walls.

Several tunnels led into the room, each one guarded by cloned dinosaurs, standing like sentinels. In the center of the chamber was a pit, ringed with long, sharp teeth-like structures jutting from its edges, as if the earth itself had grown a mouth to swallow anything that came near.

The sacred music drifted from above the pit. It was being sung by the surviving passengers, hanging grotesquely from the ceiling, suspended by strands of slime that had burrowed into their eye sockets. Their bodies were as mutilated as Rodney's, many reduced to nothing more than torsos. Only a few still clung to remnants of clothing, while the rest were left exposed, their naked forms swaying slightly in the glow. The only movement came from their mouths, which sang the haunting melody.

"Why are they singing?" I whispered. "It sounds so familiar... I *recognize* it."

"It's *O Fortuna* from Carl Orff's Carmina Burana," Shun replied. "The organism has taken control of their minds... for whatever twisted reason, it's making them sing."

As the song surged toward its thundering crescendo, Shun stepped forward, gripping one of the last grenades tightly in her hand. I hesitated, staying back, but when I saw that Shun wasn't attacked—perhaps because of the grenade in her hand—I cautiously moved to join her. The music gradually faded, leaving a chilling silence. The only sound that remained was the slow, rhythmic drip of urine falling from one of the passengers hanging from the ceiling. Then, the voices of the passengers melded into a singular, macabre chorus, their tones twisted into something otherworldly and sinister—almost demonic:

"Homo sapiens."

Shun hesitated. "Who... who are you?"

A pause followed, as if the entity was pondering its answer.

"I am God."

A cold shiver ran down my spine.

Shun leaned in, "It's likely adopting the concept most aligned with its perceived self from the survivors' minds."

The entity's chorus of voices continued, "Homo sapiens. Boundless potential."

Shun steeled herself before demanding, "Why did you bring us here?"

"Retrieved a specimen from the future," it articulated, its voice a symphony of echoes. "Assessed habitability, analyzed future genotypes. Homo sapiens identified. Such vast potential. Untapped potential."

"Potential for what?" I asked, the question trembling out of me.

The entity's communication shifted, cycling through different voices. An elderly man murmured, "Heavy machinery." A middle-aged woman declared, "Rockets." A young boy's voice added, "Space colonization," and then a child's innocent tone whispered, "Interstellar conquest." In a resonant chorus, it reiterated, "Infinite potential."

The ground trembled as two Triceratops materialized behind us, their hulking forms blocking our only exit. Shun gripped my arm tightly, her eyes flickering toward the gaping pit at the center of the room. "Let's jump," she said, tense with urgency.

Exhaustion weighed down my limbs, but the primal fear of death coursing through me kept me moving. The pit, ringed with its jagged, tooth-like protrusions, looked like anything but an escape.

"Is that even a way out?" I said, panic rising in my chest.

The entity's chorus resumed, more urgent now. "Time dwindles, Homo sapiens," it intoned before launching into a mournful rendition of *Lacrimosa*.

We leaped into the pit, its sides slick and wet, making it feel as though we were sliding down an enormous gastrointestinal tract. A rancid smell clung to the air, thick and nauseating. Halfway down, I couldn't hold it in any longer and threw up, the vomit sticking to my unkempt beard as I plummeted further into the abyss.

We found ourselves in a river of gastric acid, trapped within the pulsating walls of what seemed to be a living cave—part of the organism's biological structure. The walls throbbed rhythmically, as if they had a heartbeat.

"This is digestive fluid!" Shun shouted. "We need to get out of the water soon, or we'll be dissolved!"

The current carried us helplessly downstream, with no way to grab onto anything for escape. My skin began to burn from the acid, the stinging pain intensifying as we drifted further into the nightmarish tunnel.

"Keep your head above the surface!" Shun shouted. "You can't ingest this—it'll most likely kill you. And don't let it get in your eyes!"

I struggled to follow her instructions, gasping for air whenever my head broke through the surface of the acidic river. The current finally led us to a vast, pulsating chamber where the digestive fluid pooled. Partially digested dinosaurs floated gruesomely on the surface.

We scrambled onto a small island made of flesh, the ground beneath us slick and unnerving. Breathing was nearly impossible, as methane bubbled up from the depths of the acidic lake, filling the air with a choking, suffocating stench.

"Where are we?" I asked.

"I think we're inside a stomach," Shun replied, scanning our grotesque surroundings. "It's probably part of some kind of biological power plant."

"So, we've just thrown ourselves into the belly of the beast," I said. "How the hell are we supposed to get out?"

"Not the belly of the beast," Shun corrected, "just one of its structures."

"But how—" I began, feeling panic rise again.

"Let's stop for a moment and think," Shun interrupted, her tone calm but firm. "We need to process what it told us first."

I stood up, scanning the pulsating chamber for an exit, but there was none. "I think we need to focus on getting out of here first."

Shun remained fixated. "It gave us the final piece of the puzzle," she said, almost to herself. "It brought us back in time. A sample of the future—remember? That's what it said. It must've seen the comet ages ago, calculated its trajectory, and realized it couldn't stop it by any biological means. It couldn't reach orbit, couldn't prevent the impact... so it developed the ability to travel through time. But why did it need a sample from the future?"

"It wanted to know if the Earth would be habitable again," I said, my eyes still scanning for an exit, though I had already checked every corner.

Shun's eyes lit up with realization. "It stands to reason that if it can bring something back in time, it ought to be able to send something forward in time."

I paused, her words sinking in. "Are you saying—" I started.

"It's planning an invasion!" Shun exclaimed. "When it was talking about our species' potential, it wasn't referring to the clones it's created here. It meant the potential of our entire species. The comet is coming too soon for it to use the clones to build rockets, don't you think?"

"You're saying... it's planning to escape into the future?" I asked, my mind racing to catch up.

"Yes," Shun confirmed, her eyes widening. "That's exactly what I think it's trying to do."

A heavy silence hung between us before we both spoke at once:

"That's our ticket home!" I said, just as Shun exclaimed:

"We have to stop it!"

Her eyes narrowed in disappointment as she processed my words.

"Why must everything be our responsibility?" I asked, exasperated. "This thing doesn't stand a chance against humanity."

"Are you out of your mind?" Shun said. "We're talking about a quasi-immortal, super-intelligent organism with an arsenal of cloned dinosaurs and humans. Its knowledge and cognition are likely spread throughout its entire body—not stored in a single brain or organ we could easily destroy."

"But we've got nuclear weapons!" I insisted. "It won't stand a—"

"It might only take a small piece of it surviving to start all over again," Shun interrupted. "We need to find the mechanism that lets it travel through time and destroy it. If we do that, it won't have time to rebuild before the comet strikes."

"But... that's suicide," I said. "Please, let's just use it to hitch a ride back and—"

"We knew from the start we'd never go back," Shun implored. "I know it's worse than we imagined, Ian, but this is the sacrifice we have to make."

"Oh, God," I said, tears welling up, torn between accepting her logic and the overwhelming urge to resist it. "Maybe... maybe there's a way to survive the comet?" My words weren't driven by hope, just desperate, wishful thinking. "How far would we need to go to avoid the immediate impact?"

"I'm sure there's a way," Shun interrupted, her voice betraying the faintest tremor. "But let's focus on destroying its ability to travel through time first, okay?" Her eyes told me she didn't believe her own words. She was just saying what I needed to hear. "I have an idea," she added after a pause. "If this is a stomach, maybe... maybe we can make it vomit."

"How?" I asked, still trembling, struggling to grasp the reality of what I was contemplating—sacrificing my life for the greater good. *Ending my own life.* My mind couldn't wrap around the concept; it defied every fiber of my being. Just moments ago, the thought of traveling back home—no matter the cost—had filled me with an overwhelming sense of relief. And now, I had to let go of that last glimmer of hope, all for the sake of humanity. How could it be so easy for Shun to accept this trade, to forfeit her life for others? For me, giving up my life felt nearly impossible. But she was right, as always, and on some level, I understood what I was morally obligated to do, even if every part of me resisted it.

"The medicine we prepared for the survivors," Shun said. "It might work as an emetic drug."

She spat on the pellets, dissolving them quickly, then smeared the mixture onto the flesh beneath us. The reaction was almost immediate. The entire chamber contracted violently, and we were instantly engulfed in the gastric fluid. Caught in a whirlpool-like force, we spun around, propelled through what felt like a giant esophagus, tumbling with the rest of the acidic contents. Just as I was on the brink of drowning, we were expelled from the side of the mountain like a geyser shooting out horizontally.

Shun was lucky—she landed on a patch of soft slime tissue. I, on the other hand, slid several meters down the mountainside until I was abruptly stopped by a boulder. The impact knocked the wind out of me, with my chest taking the brunt of the blow. The pain was unbearable, especially with every breath. It nearly—though only nearly—distracted me from the agony of my other injuries. I was certain I'd broken one or two ribs.

Whimpering, I stood up, wiping the foul digestive fluid from my face and spitting it from my mouth. I reeked of vomit.

"Are you okay?" Shun asked as she carefully climbed down toward me.

Straight above us, the comet loomed behind a thin veil of clouds, its sickly green mist swirling around the bright core. It looked like a malevolent eye, silently watching over its prey.

"No!" I shouted, coughing violently, the pain in my chest flaring up so sharply that I had to lean forward. "No, I'm not okay!"

Shun's eyes widened, glancing toward the horizon. "I think it's about to happen."

"What?" I gasped, struggling to catch my breath, barely able to get the words out.

"Look, down there," she said, pointing below.

The swarm, sparkling with its luminescent blue, moved swiftly across the valley. Above it, thousands upon thousands of pterosaurs flew toward the black mountain, their wings blotting out the sky in a chaotic, frenzied migration.

"What are they doing?" I asked.

"We need to hurry," Shun replied. "They're moving into position."

"And how, exactly, are we supposed to find the structure that makes this thing travel forward in time?" I shot back. "Do you know what a biological time machine looks like? Because I sure don't!"

"Those things Rodney talked about—" Shun began.

"He wasn't making any sense!" I interrupted, my frustration spilling over. "For crying out loud, didn't you see the condition he was in? That poor, poor man."

Shun pressed on. "He used the words 'temporal,' 'crystal,' and—"

"It wasn't a sentence, Shun! It was just nonsense, fragments. He wasn't—"

"Would you shut up and listen to me?" Shun said, stomping her foot into the ground. "He said 'underground thermal energy storage.'"

"So what?" I retorted, still skeptical.

"I think the machine—if you could even call it that—is somewhere deep beneath the mountain. What else do we have to go by? It's our only lead," Shun insisted.

"Underground?" I said. "Please, no more. I can't—"

"Don't you get it, Ian?" Shun cut me off, her eyes blazing. "We're already dead. Before we even came here, we were already dead. We've been dead for sixty-six million years. The real question is: how do you want to go out? Do you want to die giving up or die trying?"

I stared at her, my eyes welling up as the weight of what awaited us beneath the mountain pressed down on me. My voice wavered as I said:

"I was in love with you."

Shun hesitated, the silence between us stretching for what seemed like an age. When she finally spoke, there was reluctance in her voice:

"I know."

We discovered an entrance a few hundred meters to our right. This time, we had little left to protect ourselves with. Shun had only two grenades, and we needed to save them for the structure below. However, the clones' preparations for their invasion of the future worked to our advantage. Most of them were occupied, moving into position atop the slime-covered ground, as if the super organism no longer had time to focus on us.

We spent hours walking, crawling, and climbing deeper into the caves, guided only by the faint blue glow of the slime coating the walls—barely enough light to illuminate the path ahead. The singing echoed around us, a twisted version of *Agnus Dei*, reverberating through the tunnels. As we pressed on, pale human faces fused with the slime stared lifelessly from the walls—cloned heads serving a purpose we couldn't begin to understand. Slimy, pallid human arms, protruding from the ceiling, reached down toward us like grotesque tentacles, trying to pull us into the depths of our darkest nightmares.

The deeper we descended, the darker it became, and the spectral music gradually faded. Down here, the slime no longer grew, its blue glow absent—relieving us of its constant presence but immersing us in a new, more suffocating kind of darkness. Without the light, we were trading one threat for another, and every step became a blind gamble.

After what felt like five hours, the temperature around us began to rise steadily. We were getting closer. A faint noise, like static, grew louder and louder until we had to shout to hear each other. Suddenly, Shun took off running. I struggled to keep up, not just because of my physical state, but more so because of the weight of my own mind. I was, quite literally, running toward my own death. The thought of it nearly paralyzed me, but somehow, I kept moving. *No, no, no—just turn around!* My mind screamed, but my legs wouldn't obey. There was no stopping now. I kept my eyes forward, refusing to turn around. But with every step, the voice in my head grew louder, making it harder to drown out.

As we cautiously peered around a corner, we were met with an intense, blinding light pouring from an opening at the far end of the cave. The static noise was deafening now, and the heat unbearable. It scorched my throat with every breath, and sweat poured down my body. It had to be over ninety degrees Celsius.

"Wait!" Shun shouted just as she was about to crawl forward. "There's a group standing at the opening!"

It was hard to make them out against the blinding light, but there was no doubt—a group of cloned humans stood there, guarding the entrance.

"Do you think they've seen us?" I whispered.

"Not yet!" Shun replied.

"What are you going to do?"

Without a word, she pulled the pin from one of the grenades.

"Let's pray to God this works," she said.

"Aren't we killing God?" I tried to force a smile, though fear churned within me.

She threw the grenade.

The static from the opening was so deafening that the grenade's explosion was almost inaudible. We waited for what felt like an unending span of time before daring to peer around the corner again. The figures we'd seen were gone. It had worked. But instead of relief, a surge of anxiety hit me hard—our success only meant we were now one step closer to certain death.

"Come on!" Shun shouted, cutting through my panic. "It's time!"

We sprinted toward the opening, stepping over the lifeless clones scattered around us. The blinding white light came from two colossal crystals suspended about fifteen meters below, above a pool of lava. Staring at them was like gazing directly into the sun. Narrow rock pathways connected the crystals to the walls, while thousands of slimy tendrils dangled from the ceiling, holding the crystals aloft, preventing them from sinking into the molten pool below.

"One of us will have to climb down there," Shun shouted over the roar of the static, "and place the grenade between the crystals!"

I didn't respond, waiting for her to take the lead.

"It's alright, Ian," she said. "I'll do it."

For a moment, I just stared at her, trying to grasp if she fully understood this would be the last thing she ever did. Then, I yelled, "O-okay, but how will you get down there?"

"We'll tie our clothes together and use them as a rope!" she replied, already starting to pull off her jacket.

My body trembled with fear and pain as I stripped off my clothes. The searing heat against my exposed skin made the burning rashes from earlier feel like nothing in comparison. We worked as quickly as we could, tying everything together, but it still felt like hours had passed.

"It's not enough!" Shun said. "We need more length—we'll have to tie it to one of the corpses!"

Distraught, I grabbed one of the clones by its leg, dragging it closer. Shun wasted no time, fastening the makeshift rope of clothes to the clone's ankle.

"You'll have to lower me down!" she said, her eyes steady but full of weight. "Do you think you can manage that?"

I nodded, though deep down, I wasn't sure if I actually could.

"Alright," she continued. "Just make sure to get me down on that narrow walkway."

She gripped the corpse's hand and started her descent. I held my end of the makeshift rope with all the strength I could muster, my muscles trembling under the strain. The voice in my head was deafening now, almost drowning out the static from the crystals. *Go back, save yourself!* The thought of death clawed at me, unbearable in its finality. The cessation of my existence—an inescapable horror that had stalked me relentlessly since childhood. Tears blurred my vision as Shun continued her slow descent. She was halfway down now. I looked at her, the air vibrating from the heat around her, and the thought struck me—*Why hadn't she chosen me over him?* It was absurd to be thinking about this now, but I couldn't help it. She caught the tears in my eyes, and in that moment, she saw my lips form the wretched words that slipped out: "I'm sorry."

I couldn't hear what she screamed as she plunged into the molten abyss below—mercifully, the deafening noise from the crystals drowned it out. In an instant, the flames erupted, and she vanished, swallowed whole by the lava. Rising to my feet, all I could think about was my second chance at life. Retracing my steps, I found myself running faster than I had on the way in—this time, unburdened by doubt. I wasn't running toward death anymore. I was running toward life. My hope of returning home had been reignited.

For a fleeting moment, an intrusive thought crept into my mind: *You loved her*. But I realized I had loved life more. Now, all I needed to do was find a patch of slime, cling to it, and wait for it to carry me back to my own time. As I moved further from the chamber with the crystals, my surroundings grew darker, until, before I knew it, I was enveloped in pitch black. The noise from the crystals gradually faded, leaving only the sound of my quick, ragged breaths echoing off the cold cave walls. In near-total darkness, I ran with my arms outstretched, fingertips brushing the rocky surface for guidance. Desperation gripped me as I tried to discern whether I was moving upward, but it was impossible to tell. Suddenly, I slipped, crashing face-first onto the cave floor. Groaning in pain, I forced myself back up, stumbling but determined, and kept running. I pressed on through the labyrinth, my hands brushing against the jagged, damp walls of the cave. The air was thick with staleness, each hurried breath leaving a bitter taste on my tongue. My footsteps were uneven, a frantic mix of sprinting and stumbling as I struggled to maintain balance on the rocky terrain. Every now and then, I'd come to a fork in the path, forced to make a split-second decision, relying solely on my gut feeling to guide me.

The air became colder, and a faint draft seeped through one of the tunnels, offering a glimmer of hope. I followed it, thinking it would lead me to an exit, only to reach a dead-end chamber crowded with stalactites and stalagmites. Frustrated, I backtracked and tried another route, my footsteps echoing through the confined space.

As I pressed on, I came across underground streams, the water icy and clear. I splashed through them, the cold numbing my feet. At one point, I encountered a narrow bridge formed by a fallen boulder, it's surface slick and treacherous. Without hesitation, I crossed it, the sound of rushing water below heightening my awareness of the danger. The maze felt endless. Each time I believed I'd found an exit, I only stumbled into another set of tunnels, each one identical to the last. My sense of direction was hopelessly lost, leaving me uncertain whether I was venturing deeper into the mountain or circling back to where I'd begun.

My pace slowed as fatigue took over. My legs felt like lead, and my lungs burned with each breath. In a final desperate attempt, I climbed a steep incline, hoping to gain a vantage point. When I reached the top, I scanned the area, searching for any sign of an exit. But all I saw were more tunnels, stretching endlessly in every direction. It was then that the crushing reality set in: I was lost in this underground labyrinth. As the weight of the situation pressed down on me, I slumped to the ground, utterly defeated.

"God, help me!" I yelled, and I wasn't calling out to the God I didn't believe in. "Please!"

The only answer was the hollow echo of my voice, swallowed by the silence of the caves.

After what felt like half an hour, a violent jolt shook the

ground beneath me. The tremors lasted for several minutes. *Was it the comet?* When the shaking finally subsided, I stood up, disoriented. The silence that followed was heavier, more oppressive than before. Then I noticed a faint light emanating from a direction that had been pitch dark earlier.

Clinging to a shred of hope, I slowly walked toward it, still praying it would lead me out, where I could join the creatures on the slime and escape. But as I reached the source of the light, all that hope vanished in an instant. The entire mountain had disappeared. In its place was a vast crater, as if carved out by some giant, precise hand. The comet loomed overhead, casting its green glow across the landscape. Cognimyxa dominator was gone.

Full of shame, I trudged through the forest and back across the valley. With no other destination in mind, I returned to the subway car, where now, I wait for death. Inside, I discovered a backpack, left behind by one of the passengers on the day we arrived. Among its contents was this notebook, where for the past week, I've been writing this testimony—my confession.

Just moments ago, the comet pierced the atmosphere, hurtling across the sky at twenty kilometers per second, bound for what will one day become Mexico. The deafening roar of its fiery descent echoed through the heavens. Shun's voice plays over and over in my mind: *We've been dead for sixty-six million years. The real question is: how do you want to go out?*

Once again, she had been right.

I know what comes next. The comet will strike with unimaginable force, and though the impact will be far to the south, the devastation will sweep across the continent. The shockwave will tear through the valley like a vengeful god, flattening everything in its path. And even as the ground trembles beneath me, even as the sky turns dark with fire and ash, I won't be able to fully accept what's happening. My mind will cling to some desperate hope, some illusion of survival. When the shockwave reaches me, I'll be paralyzed by fear. My face will twist in an expression of pure horror, and I'll instinctively press this notebook against the window. I know this because I've already seen it—the man entombed inside the mineralized subway car, forever frozen in time… that man was me.

POSTFACE

We used a three-dimensional laser scanner to examine the thin layers within the rectangular item excavated next to the remains of Dr. Ian Foster. It revealed the regular, consistent shapes of letters on each layer. Put together, like a puzzle with thousands of pieces, the testimony above appeared on our computer screens.

Dr. Foster dated their arrival in The Late Cretaceous to somewhere during the month of May and given his recollection of the events leading up to the temporal relocation it is reasonable to assume it happened—will happen—this year. The subway car Balthazar is still in transit within the Stockholm metro, so we know it hasn't happened yet.

Due to diplomatic complications, military bureaucracy, and the almost impossible task of convincing the chain in command about the truth of these findings, there isn't enough time to launch any large-scale mission on foreign soil. Therefore, I've taken it upon myself to travel to Stockholm in an attempt to remove Dr. Foster from the train. I'm breaking the law by sharing this, but as you can probably tell—given the contents of the testimony—I need all the help I can get. If I don't succeed, Cognimyxa dominator might arrive at any moment.

Kira Calder

About the Author

Thank you for joining Tobias Malm on the thrilling journey through time in ***Persona In Strata***. Tobias is a passionate writer known for crafting immersive and thought-provoking stories that blend science fiction and adventure. His works, including ***The Cave to Another World*** and ***The Culmination of Man***, continue to explore uncharted worlds and delve into the complexities of humanity.

If you enjoyed this book, please consider leaving a review on Amazon and Goodreads. Your feedback is invaluable and helps other readers discover his work.

Stay connected with Tobias and be the first to know about his upcoming projects by visiting his official website at www.tobiasmalm.com. For exclusive content and a peek behind the scenes, join his community on Patreon at https://www.patreon.com/tobiasmalm. You can also follow him on Instagram @malmtobias and on Facebook at facebook.com/malmtobias.

www.ingramcontent.com/pod-product-compliance
Lightning Source LLC
La Vergne TN
LVHW091319150826
845673LV00006B/1701

* 9 7 8 9 1 5 3 1 2 6 6 6 9 *